The Librarian

Christy Sloat

Published by
CHBB Publishing, LLC.

Edited by Cheree Castellanos and Melanie Williams
Cover & Formatting by Pretty AF Designs

Praise for The Librarian

"This book is pure magic! A must read for any library dwelling book addict!
The Librarian has the whimsy of Alice in Wonderland, The romance of Outlander, complete with some major Time Lord responsibilities, but you can skip the Tardis for this time traveling adventure!"

-A. Giacomi, Author of The Zombie Girl Saga

"Sloat did a brilliant job of showing the sacrifice and sorrow that can sometimes accompany tragic star-crossed lovers. It's a beautiful story, expertly weaved that I highly recommend! "

- Stacey Rourke. Award Winning Author of The Legends Saga

"Mysterious, lyrical, and wonderful. Jack is the perfect book boyfriend you'll completely fall in love with!"

-SJ Davis, author of Ghost in the Machine

This one is for readers everywhere and the librarians who help us discover the magic in books.

The
Librarian

Prologue

The waves lapped upon the shore as Gram and I collected seashells. It was one of our favorite traditions to do by moonlight. With my small chubby fingers, I pulled up a perfectly intact shell.

"Look, Gram! It's beautiful," I called to her as she ambled her way toward me. She nodded and smiled. "It's going to be perfect for your collection, Emme. You shouldn't let go of the perfect ones in life."

I shrugged and kept digging until my small seven-year-old fingers were frozen from the Maine coastal winds that bore down upon us. We eventually made our way back to the library and walked up the steps to the apartment where we lived. Gram's library was a sanctuary for me. My home now. Without her needing to tell me, I ran a bath and washed the sand from my body and hair. After I was done, I dressed myself in the warmest pajamas I could find. Gram sat at the table drinking tea and kissed me as I approached.

"You're growing so fast, Emme. Your parents would be proud of you." I smiled, not sure how they'd know if I was doing well or not. I saw our shells drying on the counter, knowing they'd be dry and put away in our jars by the morning.

"Now off to bed with you," Gram told me as she playfully tugged my hair. I kissed her cheek and went to my room.

During the night, something woke me from a deep sleep. I sat up hearing whispered voices from somewhere outside my room. I padded across the floor, being careful not to wake Gram, and peeked outside my door. Nothing.

Opening my door wider didn't reveal the noise either. I grabbed my robe, knowing just where to look. I had to be fast or she'd catch me, so I swiftly went out the door of our apartment, down the stairs, and into the library. The noise got louder and revealed a man's voice.

As I got closer to the small room where Gram did her important paperwork, I saw a man standing with Gram. He was handsome and tall compared to my gray-haired, short Gram. She slumped into her chair and he remained standing.

"Well, what if I don't want that future for her? Do I not have any say in the matter?"

He rubbed his chin. His back was now facing me, and it was then that I noticed his peculiar type of attire. He wasn't wearing clothes that normal men wore; in fact I had never seen anyone wear pants like his. He looked like an explorer from one of my books with his pants tucked neatly inside of his boots.

"I'm afraid neither of us has a say; it's entirely up to Emmeline. If she grows up and begins reading the books, then she will know whether or not she wants to do it. You mustn't hold her back from her legacy."

They were talking about me! I crouched down, hiding in the shadows, hoping to figure out *what* they were discussing.

As it was, I was so confused.

"You can't make her protect them, Harold. She will have a choice. She's my granddaughter!" Gram was angry now, and no one wanted to be around her when she was like that.

Harold backed up a step and slowly took off his funny hat. "I know how you feel—"

Gram snorted. "No, you do not. I have lost my son and his wife. I will not lose her. It is too dangerous. She will have a different life than that."

"Your son didn't die because of the gift, Mavis. And you cannot travel. But it *will* go to her and you know it. Someday you will no longer be here, and she will have to protect your legacy."

She made another noise with her nose and said, "My legacy wasn't something I chose, thanks to you, Harold. I think you meant well, but you and I both know how dangerous this is. Traveling through time to protect history isn't something that—" She stopped abruptly and focused her eyes onto where I was currently crouched. "I think we have company."

I froze. She could see me. I wasn't as hidden as I thought I was. And Gram was always good at seeing me when I thought I was being sneaky.

"Emmeline, come here."

With wobbly legs I walked into my Gram's forbidden office, and Harold never turned around to meet my gaze. Instead, he stood still and faced only Gram.

"What have I told you about sneaking around at night?" Gram asked sternly.

"Umm...not to," I said shakily, almost in tears.

"Now get your tushy back upstairs and into bed." I did as she said, never once looking at the man in the eyes.

As I walked back to my room, my brain tried hard to figure out what they were speaking about. Traveling through time? Legacy? It was confusing for a seven-year-old to know what those words meant. I would ask her about it in the morning. If I didn't have the nerve to do that, then I would look it up in the library.

But as I felt sleep pull me back under, I had already forgotten the whole conversation and the words in which I was to learn.

One

I set out to run the path around my dorm's building after my long day in class. It was my release after being swarmed with lecture after lecture and being forced to read books I didn't want to read. The lights from the street lamps lit my way as I ran along the curvy trail. I didn't want to stay out here too late. We did, after all, have a huge day planned for tomorrow. As I ran, all the things we had to do to set up tomorrow's run filled my mind along with the stress of finishing up my year at Berkley. I would be sad to leave my friends behind, but England was calling to me. I had this all worked out for years, and it was finally within my grasp. I looked forward to finishing up the rest of my college life and becoming a teacher. I could actually see it play out in front of me like a movie. So far, it went as planned. I spent my one year here in California, and I joined a sorority, got great grades, and made new friends. I would stay in England perhaps and teach there if I wanted. I was only nineteen and had accomplished so much already. It helped that I took accelerated classes in high school, giving me extra credits. The only downside to that was missing out on actual teen-life. I didn't date then nor did I have a lot of friends. I made up for that here at Berkley though.

I wouldn't be stuck in Bay Ridge like everyone I graduated with. I would be living abroad. I would have tea in the mornings and in the afternoons. I wouldn't be suffering freezing temperatures like I grew up with in Maine, choosing not to be subjected to a life on the Maine coast any longer.

Saving all of my money, I got grants so I could go to school. I did everything with the focus that in the end I would be happy. I wouldn't be like Gram, not that being like her was a terrible thing, but I wouldn't be the town librarian. She had hoped that I would take the reins after she retired and I would take over the library. But I just couldn't see myself sitting at a desk and re-shelving books every day. Gram was good at her job. She read to the kids every Tuesday, and she helped the seniors every Thursday. She got three computers for the library and set them up so people in Bay Ridge could actually have Internet. That's another thing I didn't miss. The service there was terrible.

Taking the corner at high speed, I felt my muscles tighten up as I ran faster and faster. There was always this feeling of exhilaration while I ran. I craved it on stressful days, like my muscles yearned for the torture the run put them through. I sighed as I felt the burn in my legs, and at the same time my stress sort of melted away. The study session I had with Harmony was gone out of my mind for just a second. Then a guy came out of nowhere, and I crashed into him with a smack.

He fell, actually he tumbled, and I smacked my face on the grass.

"Oh my God, are you all right?" He laughed.

He held out a hand, and I took it as he pulled me up and

my face burned with embarrassment. I was really tired, and no matter how graceful I was as a runner, I always seemed to hurt myself when I ran after a long day. I brushed off my knees and the guy did the same. Thankfully I fell face first into the grass, not the concrete.

"I think I'll live. But these yoga pants are done for," I told him as I stuck my finger through the large hole at the knee. I looked up, and as the street light shone down on his face, I could see him fully. He was gorgeous, and I recognized him. I'd seen him around and drooled over his hot body a few times.

"I'm Emme by the way. Sorry for running into you."

I pulled my hair back off of my sweaty face and gathered it into a high ponytail. I suddenly wished I wasn't standing in front of him so grossly slick with sweat. He didn't seem to mind, though, as he checked me out.

"I'm Eric, and you can run into me anytime you want. You belong to Alpha Chi Beta, don't you?"

"Yep." I was proud of my sorority and even prouder that he knew I was part of them. "Are you coming tomorrow?"

He nodded, and I knew a guy like him would be up early to watch the 5k we had put together. Of course any guy who wasn't there was a complete idiot or not into girls.

"The Undie 5k is a great idea," he said eagerly. "I can't wait." *I bet he couldn't.*

It really was a genius idea. Harmony was the one who came up with it. Once we started sign-ups, at least half of the student body was there begging to sign up. Girls wanted to strip down to their panties so that they could show off their assets and hopefully gain the attention of some guy they were hopelessly pining for. The guys were there checking out the hot girls who would be stripping down and running in their skivvies. We made sure it was only a girl run. That was my idea. No guys in their tighty-whities would be running. No one needed to see guys junk flopping around as they ran. No thank you. The event was limited to only female students who were participating and anyone that donated to the run, we made sure. We were using the money for our sorority and donating fifty percent to cancer research. We had made bank on this run, and I was proud that we were sending quite a bit to the fund.

As much as I hoped to run the 5k, I had to work it. Although, I would still be stripping down to my undies; it was the one thing Dawn insisted we make a requirement for all of us. We had to be in our undies so we showed the school that we were like them. So many people thought all sorority girls were snotty bitches—granted some were—but not all of them. I agreed to strip knowing that someday I would look back and hopefully laugh about these days. Besides, what is college for if not to have fun and be a little reckless?

"Will I see you there?" Eric asked me with a smile.

I nodded and bit my lip. I hadn't really let myself get too attached to guys here. Sure some girls want relationships, but I wasn't ready for that, especially since I was leaving soon.

"Yeah, I'll be there. Come by and see me," I said as I backed away from him slowly.

He nodded and said, "I can't wait."

I ran back to the dorm, ignoring the pain in my knees. I could feel Eric's eyes on me as I ran. I made sure to run slowly so that he could see me better. I wasn't afraid of flirting; I actually liked it. It was fun to meet a guy and hang out and maybe, if the timing was right, hook up. I was all for meeting new people. I wasn't ready for a serious relationship. It seemed I was at the right school for that since none of the guys I had met called or even hinted at a date after things got physical. It didn't ever hurt my feelings. I was here on a temporary basis only and didn't need any loose ends to tie up before I went to England. I already had Gram calling me every week, asking me when I was coming home. I could just imagine how awful a long distance relationship would be.

I reached the dorm, and by then my knee was aching so badly that I was seriously limping. I opened my door and found Harmony and Dawn, my sorority sisters, fighting over which panty and bra set to wear tomorrow.

"I already told you I like the blue, now you're trying to get me to like the gold," Harmony accused. "Gold is for hookers, and we, my friend, are not hookers."

I laughed. Harmony was my hippie friend. She was into free love and peace, but not selling her body. Her name fit her personality for sure.

Getting her to agree to wear the underwear was like pulling teeth. Finally she gave in when she realized it was for a good cause. She's a sucker for those.

"Harmony, you don't like gold? Fine, but I hate the blue. We'll have to go out and exchange these for a different color," Dawn huffed putting her hand on her hip. I knew Dawn's tactic here, and I stood back to see what Harmony would do. Harmony hated shopping malls and everything they stood for. I bit my lip and watched her face, waiting.

She looked from the pile of underwear to me and back again. She threw her hands up and said, "Fine! Let's go to the mall."

My mouth fell open in shock. I couldn't believe she chose that over the gold underwear. Dawn picked them up and found the receipt inside her purse, then turned to me and said, "Get dressed, Emme. We're going shopping."

I saluted her and found a new pair of comfy yoga pants. My limp was getting worse by the time we got to the car.

"What the hell is wrong with your leg?" Dawn asked in irritation.

"I fell, but it's okay because I fell into this hot guy. So I hurt myself for a good reason," I explained. They stared at me, then burst out laughing like I said the funniest joke they'd ever heard.

"Only you could make hurting yourself sound fun," Dawn said.

We piled into the car and drove to the mall. It was a quick fifteen minute ride from our campus if we took the highway, which we did. Luckily, since it was now dark, the mall was dead. Dawn pulled the car into a handicapped space, and I shook my head as she pulled out her grandpa's card and hung it onto the mirror.

"What?" she asked, feigning ignorance. She pointed to my knee and said, "You're injured."

After limping through most of the mall, we finally made it to the lingerie store. I could stay in there all day smelling perfume and picking out cute undies. I had a thing for adorable underwear. I liked to look sexy, and there was nothing wrong with that.

"How about pink?" I asked holding up a pale pink panty and bra set.

Both girls shook their heads and argued over a floral pattern. I sighed and looked up and found a black and hot pink set that stood out and practically begged me to take it home. I reached out and ran my fingers over the lacey pattern. It was beautiful and so my style.

"This...this right here," I told the girls. They stopped bickering and stopped to stare.

"Wow, you really have a passion for shopping," Harmony said quietly.

"No, Harmony, my passion isn't for shopping. I have an eye for beautiful things, and this is beautiful," I explained. I felt a slight buzz in my pocket—my phone.

I pulled it out and answered right away. The caller was my best friend from back home, Rose.

"Rose, what's up?"

She sighed, and I could hear a tremble in her voice. "Your Grandma Mavis is here. They brought her in via ambulance, Emme."

I dropped the bra and panties and backed out of the store slowly as if getting away from the beautiful things would lessen the heart-pounding fear that I felt at that moment.

"Is...is she all right?" My voice cracked, and I knew instantly it was a stupid question.

You know when you feel the bad news is *real* bad? Like when you get that call in the middle of the night and you know it's not good news because it's so late at night and who would be calling you? The fear of the answer Rose had for me was tightening around my throat like a noose.

"It's her heart, Emme. It's growing weary. She was complaining of shortness of breath. She called me instead of 911, stubborn woman. So I dispatched an ambulance right away." Rose was a doctor at Bay Ridge Regional, our town's only hospital, and was always there for my Gram when she needed help. "She is experiencing heart failure."

She was doing that thing she did ever since she became a doctor; she was talking to me like a patient. I absolutely hated it. I didn't like to be babied, especially by my best friend.

"Shit, Rose, spit it out. What the hell is going on?"

"She's dying, and if you want to say your goodbyes, then

get your ass on a plane as soon as you can."

"Okay," I whispered and hung up. I looked at my friends and tears slipped down my face unexpectedly. "My Gram is sick. I have to go."

Two

My leave of absence was emailed and approved by noon the next day, which was great timing since I found a flight leaving at three. I packed a small carry-on bag, thinking my stay wouldn't be too long. I packed a week's worth of clothes and my necessities into the bag: laptop, toiletries, make-up, and reading material. My hands shook as I slid the zipper closed. I stopped packing and took a breath, willing them to stop, but they didn't listen.

Harmony and Dawn were at the sorority house celebrating the awesome 5k they put on. Instead of participating that morning, I had been busy typing my leave of absence email and talking to Rose about Gram's steady decline. She was now in ICU and in a coma. Rose swore up and down that she was comfortable, but I couldn't imagine Gram being comfortable with tubes down her throat and in her arms. I shivered at the thought of seeing her like that.

Gram was tough as nails. She was raised in Maine, and her family lived in a small cabin that did not have indoor plumbing, a heater, or air conditioning. Her family stayed warm by a fire on cold nights and cooled down at the lake on hot summer days. She always told me stories about growing up in that small cabin.

"All five of us would share a room," she'd explain. "My mother and father had their own room, but us kids had to share. I didn't mind at all. I liked sleeping together with them, especially in the winter. We would snuggle up and stay toasty that way."

Her accent was thick, just like most of the townspeople. Our town was a well-known fishing and harbor town, and most passersbys would remark on how funny we spoke. Gram would tell them that no one talked funny but the flatlanders— her name for all non-Maine folks—and they'd laugh like they knew what she meant.

I took my bag and heaved it over my shoulder. I left a note for the girls and didn't look back at my room. I would be back to see it soon. Gram would recover, and I would come back and finish school. Then my plans would remain. My life was just on pause.

****

The plane made a soft humming sound when we reached our altitude, and I was thankful for it. The constant engine noise was grating on my nerves. I pulled out a book that Gram had given me, and I held it in my hands caressing the cover. It brought back a memory of reading in Gram's library.

Her building was not always a library. Before Gram bought it, which was years before I was born, it was the home of Mr. Harold Lockhart. Harold was a scientist, and the house was befitting of a man of science. It was built very strangely. The top half was his private home and the bottom his lab and perfume store.

I always thought it was strange that a scientist would also sell perfume, but Gram told me that he sold other things. Then, as a child, I never understood fully what she had meant. But now as a grown woman I knew that Mr. Lockhart would sell medicinal supplies and probably things no doctor would ever prescribe. From what I understood, he was a very profound and admired scientist until his death in the late seventies. It was before his death that he gave Gram the house. At first, she moved in to the top and sold books in the bottom half. Gram had always had a love affair with books. She told me once that she loved books more than my grandpa loved the sea. He owned his own fishing boat, and it was there that he spent a lot of his time. I never met him because the summer of 1987 he died at sea, leaving my dad fatherless and Gram a widow.

She then turned the book store into a library. Times were hard in Bay Ridge and people had a hard time buying books. Gram decided our town needed the written word, so she became the only town librarian. She was needed in our boring town. I grew up there and relied on books as my escape from harsh winters and hot boring summers. I know most of the town relied on her then, and still did.

My eyes began to close, and instead of diving into the pages of my book, I fell asleep.

"Folks, I'd like to let you know we have reached the Bangor airport. It's a cold night out there, so be sure to bundle up," the Captain said, waking me from a dream. I wiped my mouth and felt drool on my chin. I looked around and noticed most people did the same. Oh well, I guess I wasn't the only drooler on this flight. I looked out of the window and noticed the snowy ground below. It sure wasn't great to be back. I left California and it was seventy degrees, and I come here and it's literally freezing. Fabulous.

I departed the plane and found a rental car company that was willing to rent a car to someone my age. The girl behind the desk handed me keys to a small two door car. Was she kidding me?

"I need an SUV; it's snowing outside!" I informed her as she rolled her eyes. I know it had been years since I had driven in the snow, but I could have handled the roads. I just didn't want to drive a small compact car in this crap.

She typed something and informed me there was a bigger car on the lot.

"Great! I'll take it."

As I stood staring at the minivan, I literally ate my words.

"Shit," I said to myself. I climbed in and started up the mommy-van. To my surprise it ran pretty smooth as I made my way onto the interstate. I wouldn't be racing anyone anytime soon, but it took the snowy roads pretty well.

As I watched the snow fall around me and kept an eye out for moose on the road, I was reminded of the day my parents died. The night was so similar. I was tucked into bed while Gram babysat me so my parents could go out on a much needed date.

They hadn't been on one in so long, and I can still remember my mom asking Gram if she wouldn't mind watching me. I brushed my Barbie's hair while Mom did hers in a pretty bun. Her black hair always hung down around her face, so to see her face for once, free of hair, was so amazing.

"Mommy, you're beautiful," I had told her.

She scooped me up and said, "But you are more beautiful and fairer than any in the land." My mom always told me stories of distant lands where princesses lived and waited for their prince. In all of the stories, I was the princess. "Now come on. We have to get you to Gram's."

The roads weren't bad that night, not from my recollection, but the snow was heavy. My mom and dad looked so happy as I watched them get into their car and wave goodbye to me. I waved back, not knowing that I would never see them again. Gram became my mom and dad in one night. She took me in and cared for me after they died, and I'll never forget how she remained so strong. Even after the funeral when I would cry, she'd say, "You're mom and dad are not gone forever. You'll see them again someday. No crying because you must be strong and live this life that they gave you. You are a gift, and they would want you to live each day thankful for what you have and who you will someday be."

I'll never forget her words, and I still didn't. As I made my way to Bay Ridge, I wondered how in the world a strong woman like Gram could leave this world. My Gram was tough, no one else in our town was tougher. I knew she would be just fine and make it out of the hospital and back into the library soon. She just needed to get her heart fixed, that's all.

My phone buzzed at that same moment.

"Rose?" I answered with my freezing hands.

"Where are you, Emme? The weather is getting kind of rough here," she said.

"I'm about an hour out. How is Gram doing?"

"Emme, she's not getting any better. She is still in a coma. We're doing all we can to make her comfortable, but she has strict rules for how she wants to spend her last days. I need you to get here so we can discuss them."

Ugh, she was doing that doctor thing again.

"Rose, I know you're trying to prepare me and all, but I have a feeling Gram will be fine."

"Emme," Rose whispered, "I don't think you understand

the severity of the situation. Your gram isn't going to get better. She is declining, and she asked us not to keep her alive on machines. I mean, don't you understand what I'm saying to you?"

Anger coursed through me now as I gripped the steering wheel. I tried really hard not to lose it on Rose, but I didn't think she understood. She had parents still, who she saw every day.

"Rose, I understand. I'm not a child, but I'm trying to stay positive. Do you think this is easy for me? I'm losing the last family member I have left. I'll be...I'll be *alone*." I pulled the car into a turnout and took heavy breaths as the tears threatened to come. "I need to go. I can't focus on the road while I cry." I hung up on my friend and got back on to the road. I had to get to Gram and make sure she made it through this.

Three

Finally I made it to Bay Ridge and saw the welcome sign even through the heavy snow. I could instantly smell the salty air as I rolled down the window. It had been a long time. I had to smell it, but the snow was getting in and all over me so I rolled it back up.

Turning onto the main road, I saw the hospital leering in front of me.

Dread. I felt it as I got closer. The town was asleep as it usually was this early in the morning. The sun was just coming up over the roofs of the buildings and houses.

It was a small town. There were only three traffic lights, but it was growing. I could see that as I drove through. There was a coffee shop that hadn't been there before and a new sandwich shop. As I turned the corner to the hospital, I saw new construction going in. They had levelled out quite a bit of forest to build God-only-knows-what. The sign read: JR Builders, bringing you brighter tomorrows.

"Ugh," I moaned. The last thing the town needed was a strip mall. Sure, the little kids here would enjoy a new movie theatre and bowling alley, but would they really like a new mall?

Just by thinking that made me a traitor. I had packed up and moved away as soon as I graduated, and my new life was surrounded by buildings and malls. I had left this small town behind, and now I wasn't in the position to say what was right or wrong. I was an outsider now.

I pulled into the hospital parking lot and parked the van. Stretching my legs felt so good as I walked into the main entrance. I felt fine until I saw Rose coming to meet me. As soon as I saw her face, I lost it, falling into her arms and crying. She cried too as she held me tightly. I didn't know how much I missed my friend until that moment. We talked frequently, but I didn't realize she would look so damn grown up.

"I'm so sorry if I sounded insincere earlier. I just ..." she sobbed softly. "I just didn't want you to think the impossible." She pulled away from me and looked me in the eyes. "She's dying, Emme. We've removed a lot of the tubes, to make her comfortable."

I nodded and didn't say a word because what could I say? There were no words that would save Gram, and I had come here hoping beyond hope that Gram would pull through.

I followed her to ICU and wiped my tears with the back of my hand. The hospital was quiet, save for a few beeps and nurses talking.

Rose opened the door to the ICU and in we went. My hands were betraying me as they shook nervously. There lay Gram on the first bed to my right.

I wasn't prepared to see Gram's frail body spread out on the tiny hospital bed. Her once black and gray hair was now as white as snow. Her strong face was slack and pale. Her once firm hands were covered with tubes and looked gray.

Her color was all wrong. She was bright and lively the last time I saw her; now she was faded.

She looked dead already, and a chill went through me at seeing her like this. When my parents died in the car accident, I never had to see them like this. My last thoughts of them were vibrant and alive. Now my last moments with Gram would not be. Would I always think of this moment when I thought of her?

I rushed to her side and held her hand gently, afraid she would break. I rubbed her hand tenderly, and for the first time ever I was wracked with the guilt of leaving her here alone. When I left a year ago, I didn't look back. I was so selfish. How could I leave her here? She had no one to take care of her, and when she needed me most, I was shopping for underwear.

I hated myself in that moment, and it showed on my face because Rose grabbed me by the shoulders and said, "Now you knock that shit off right now, Emme. She wasn't alone. She has the whole town here supporting her."

"But, I left her. She was there when I was alone and parentless, and I left her. When she needed me, I was out in California being a pretentious little shit."

Rose shook her head and laughed.

"You went away to school. I did too; I left. I was gone way longer than you were."

It wasn't the same, and she knew it. She went to school one state away and was home on weekends with her family. Rose was older than I was and of course had her career before me. When she went to college, I knew I wanted to go too. I always wanted to teach abroad and had a plan by my sophomore year. So when I graduated, I packed up my car and left this small town behind, and Gram too.

A nurse came in and interrupted our talk, but I didn't mind. She whispered a few things to Rose, and her eyes grew wide.

"When did this happen?" Rose asked suddenly.

"When you were downstairs on break," the nurse said hesitant.

Rose came to Gram's bedside and checked her vitals and quickly flashed a light in her eyes. My heart was pounding as she did so. I was terrified at what this was all about.

"What is it?" I asked frantically.

"She said while I was downstairs, Mavis woke up and called out for you. She must be coming out of the coma." Now my heart was really pounding. Could Gram possibly be getting better? Or was it a fluke. I had read once that when the body is dying the brain did strange things.

"Talk to her, Emme. She will hear you. She's not brain dead; she's just not strong enough to fight anymore," Rose instructed me.

I leaned in and sat next to her body. It felt cold, so I pulled the blanket up higher. I ran my hands over her hair and said, "I'm here, Gram. I came all the way home. I won't leave you again." I cried and the tears slipped onto her. "I'm so sorry for leaving. I never intended to leave you alone. I only wanted to go to school." I paused, waiting for her to wake up and reply to me. I shot a glance at Rose, and she ushered me to go on.

"I was driving here, and I was thinking about all the times we spent together in the library and how special you have made my life here. I can't lose you, Gram. I'm not ready." The sobs took over, and I bent down to cry. If I never got to hear her voice again, I would never forgive myself.

I felt her hand reach up and run through my hair. Looking up, I saw her dark brown eyes stare at mine. I smiled lightly.

She returned the smile and said, "Don't you ever say foolish things, child. You've been my delight for all of these years. I'm so proud of you." She stopped and coughed a horrible liquid sounding cough. Her eyes didn't hold their usual light. She looked exhausted.

"She may have fluid in her lungs," Rose said as she rushed to Gram's side to do God-knows-what.

"No!" Gram said, hoarsely. "Enough. I'm ready to die." She coughed again and seeing her like this was tearing me apart. "I don't want to be in anymore pain. Just let me go."

I looked at Rose and had no idea what to do. She was obviously hurting with each cough.

"I can give you something for the pain, but Mavis, if you don't let me clear that fluid, you'll ..."

"I'll drown and die like my husband. So leave me be. I've signed my papers." Gram had signed her DNR papers, but that didn't mean Rose had to stand by and not treat her symptoms.

"Gram, Rose has a duty to treat your symptoms while you're here. She can't let you drown in your own fluid. What if you can make it out of this and go home?" I was always hopeful.

Gram's eyes fluttered and Rose went to work. I stepped back and fell into the nurse's arms as she ushered me out of the room so they could work. I couldn't help but wonder if I would get a proper chance to say goodbye.

****

I woke up an hour or so later and blinked my eyes to find I was still in the waiting room, alone. Rose hadn't come out to talk to me yet. I pulled myself upright and dug for my phone.

There were no missed calls, so I shut it back down and threw it in my bag.

The sun was all the way up in the sky, and I stretched. I needed to see what was going on with Gram, but there was no one to talk to. I found a coffee machine and made myself a cup with extra sugar and no cream, because there wasn't any. I braved the coffee and was surprised that it was good.

"There you are, Sleeping Beauty," Rose said as she walked into the room. "I figured since we got your Gram settled and rested, I'd let you sleep."

I put the coffee down and ran my hands over my messy head. "Can I see her?"

Rose nodded and took me down the hall. I wondered then if she ever slept.

"When do you go home?" I asked her.

She laughed. "That's a funny joke. *Home,* what's that?"

I stopped her in the hall. "Wait, are you telling me you don't go home? Come on."

"I do. I just haven't been there in two days. Not since Mavis came in. I'm one of three doctors in this hospital and the only one who specializes with the care she needs. I'm the only one you'd want to take care of her, right?" I nodded. "So that's why I stay: for you."

I wrapped her in my arms and thanked her for staying. "Is Gram stable?"

She nodded. "For now. We've moved her from ICU to her own room. She is comfortable. She asked that I give her something for the pain, but she is awake. The pulmonary edema has subsided for now, but with her weak heart it will either come back or her heart will give out."

I bit my lip and wondered out loud, "How long does that give her?"

"It's hard to say, maybe two days or maybe a week. I know that she won't make it home, Emme. But that's what she's been asking for, to die in her bed. I just can't release her to go home. Without the proper comforts, she would be in a lot of pain. Even a woman as tough as her, she wouldn't be able to die at home."

I understood what she meant, Gram would be in so much pain and we'd end up back here anyway. I followed her to a nice quiet room where Gram lay. She actually had a bit more color in her cheeks, but nothing like the Gram I knew. I sat with her as she slept until it got dark. Finally when I couldn't sit there any longer or read anymore magazines, I left the hospital to go home and shower. I had been in the hospital for almost twenty-four hours.

Rose had gone home to sleep, and the hospital staff knew I was only down the road and to call me if Gram woke up. They gave me a bag of Gram's belongings as I left the hospital.

I drove the small trek to the library. I didn't expect to feel what I did when I pulled into the lot. All of the feelings of home came back to me. The times I would run around the library like it was my playground, the summers spent on the beach across the street, and Gram's face while I made snowmen in the parking lot.

The old building was a faded robin's egg blue that needed to be re-painted from the many storms that hit our coast. But it was built sturdy and strong just like Gram.

I put my key in the lock and pushed the door in. Snow had built up on the steps, and I shoveled it away and poured salt on it so I didn't slip coming out in a rush to go back to the hospital. A pile of mail sat at the hardwood floor when I walked into the entrance. I pulled them from the floor and set them aside for another time. I looked around the library for a moment. It sat to the left when you entered the door and had its own entrance. To the right was a separate door that led up a few stairs to Gram's house. The library was quiet as I opened the other door. I shut it and walked up the creaky steps. It was a miracle she never fell down and broke a hip on the damned stairs.

The house was clean as usual and still smelled of lemon. The white walls were filled with pictures of me from my childhood. I passed them by without a second glance.

The kitchen needed a few groceries and a good mopping. Something had spilled on the floor, maybe milk, and was now sticky. I didn't want to think how the spill happened, but I was sure it happened when she called Rose.

I went to my old bedroom, and it felt so very strange to be home. I set my bag down and Gram's next to it. Digging out my pajamas, I went to my bathroom to clean up. Once inside I took a good long look at myself.

I looked like shit. My brown hair was frizzy and pulled up in the worst ponytail possible. I had always loved the color of my hair, but hated my curls. I wished that I had straight hair like Rose or my friends back home. Oh, how easy ponytails and showers would be. Not to mention the money I would save on product. My make-up was smeared under my eyes like I had stayed out partying all night.

I started the shower and let the heated mist surround me as I cleaned away the sadness and the stress.

When I emerged, I checked my phone; no missed calls. I wasn't sure if that was a good thing or not. I needed to nap and to get my butt back to see Gram. But as I put on my sweatpants and T-shirt, it was the library that called to me. I listened to the call and walked down the stairs and into my Gram's library. I turned on the lights and a heavy feeling came over me. What would happen to this place when Gram died? I wasn't sure, but one thing I did know was that I was not the person for the job.

Four

I left the thought of who would take Gram's place at the door and walked the aisles and browsed the books. There were so many books in this old library. For such a small place, it held a lot of literature. I came to the end of the last stack and found my favorite spot in the whole space: a special reading nook just for me. It was where I would spend my days off of school while Gram worked. When I wasn't playing with friends, I was here cuddled up reading. It looked the same as it did when I was small, except it was tiny now. I didn't remember it being so small. I bent down through the small door and into the room where a rocking chair sat in one corner. In the opposite corner Gram put in a fake fireplace that just blew heat instead of burning real logs. I turned it on and sat on the window seat that was full of comfy blankets and pillows. It looked out to the ocean across the street. The snow had stopped and I could see far out at sea. There were ships coming to port, and it amazed me that while Gram was dying, life was still moving on.

I searched the bookshelves for my favorite set of books when my phone started to buzz. I answered hastily, "Hello?"

"Emme, it's me. You need to come." It was Rose, and she was sounding serious again.

"Be there in two." I hung up and left the library, lights on and all.

I parked the van and ran into the hospital. I didn't know what I was going to face inside, but I would do it knowing that Gram's memory would live on. I wouldn't let her library go away; I would find someone to take care of it.

I came to her room, and Rose stopped me before I went in.

Her face was ashen, and she looked dead tired.

"Emme, you need to be with her now. Just say your goodbyes."

"I thought she was awake and out of the woods, Rose? What happened in the two hours I was gone?"

She bit her lip. "Her heart is weak, and it's giving out. I've done all that I can."

I pushed past her and mumbled, "Two days." She said I would have more time, and she was wrong.

Gram wasn't sitting up and smiling like I had hoped she would have been. Instead she was lying on her back and staring off into space. When I came in, she noticed me and smiled, weakly.

"Gram!" I practically ran into her arms. She lifted them and tried to wrap them around me, and I stifled a cry. "I'm here."

Her voice was weak and frail and nothing like earlier. "I'm dying. I feel it. I need you to listen to me, Emmeline." I nodded and leaned back to stare into her watery eyes.

"I'm listening, Gram."

"Emmeline, you are my only descendant, and I need you to do something for me."

I cried, "Anything."

"I need you to take care of my library. I want you to make sure those assholes don't take it," she coughed.

"Who, Gram?"

"The builders. They wanna bulldoze her and put up shopping malls. Don't let them."

I nodded even though I didn't fully comprehend what was happening with the builders.

"I also want you to understand that you *have* to become the librarian. Not anyone else." She was gravely serious, and I didn't give any hints that this was against my wishes and future plans. "No one else can do it. And I don't mean that they can't handle it, I mean they don't have the blood for it. The library is special. It's magic. And only you can take over for me because of your blood."

"I don't understand, but I'm still listening," I told her honestly.

Her voice became barely a whisper, and she spoke in between horrible coughs of fluid.

"There is a set of books, and only you can touch them. I'm serious now, Emmeline. No one must touch these books, understand?" I nodded again. "You'll find them under my desk in the floorboards. I want you to read them. Read them, whenever you can, but just read them."

I nodded and then asked, "Why are the books important? Are they our family history?"

I had always wondered about our family history. Where we all came from and who my ancestors were. Gram shook her head once.

"No, child, they're not our family history. But they are important to our family. I know this doesn't make a lick of sense right now, but it will. The puzzle pieces will all fall into place. The books don't work for me; I'm unable to enter them. I think if you take over the library they'll work for you." It was then that she opened her hand and inside was her mother's wedding ring. She shakily placed it into my hand. I glanced down at the ring and fondly back to her. "I love you."

"I love you too, Gram. I'm sorry I left you," I cried. I wanted to say more, but she stopped me.

"No. Don't be sorry. You had to. Now I have to go. My time is up, darling. Please do as I say, and don't let them take my library," she begged.

I nodded and she smiled. She clenched my hands and I said, "I promise, Gram."

She went into a strange quiet faze, where she breathed slowly for what seemed like hours, but could have been minutes.. Her lungs gurgled and her heart barely beeped on the monitor. All I thought about was our times together and the happiness she brought into my life when I had none.

I felt her body move, and she took a deep breath in and exhaled all of the air in her lungs and didn't breathe in again after that. My Gram died in my arms with her eyes closed like a sleeping angel. Alarms sounded as her heart stopped, and Rose came into the room to shut them off. She put her arms around me and held me tightly.

****

One week later I sat in Gram's kitchen, which was mine now. Gram left the whole property to me in her will, along with her money, jewels, and truck. I didn't want any of it. I wanted her back.

I had shut down the library and the town understood. The Reich's sent a casserole and the Odell's a peach pie. More people sent food, but I couldn't bring myself to eat anything. My friends from college sent text messages asking when I'd be back to school, but I didn't respond. They never once asked how Gram was or what happened. All they cared about was when I would be back and ready to party again.

Rose came by and made me shower because she said I stunk up Gram's beautiful house. I put on a brave face, but when she left, I broke down.

Truth was I wasn't strong. I didn't know how to live in Maine, in Gram's home, without Gram. Sure, send me to California, back to school, and I could live because then I wouldn't be faced with it. I wouldn't have Gram's words rolling around in my head all the time.

"You have to become the librarian. Not anyone else."

"It's magic."

"Don't let them take it."

"There are a set of books ..."

My questions went unanswered. I wondered why these books were so important to Gram and why *I* had to be the only one to run this damn library. Why is it a blood thing? I wondered what was special about these books that I had to protect. I couldn't even imagine what Gram was thinking before she passed, but to talk to me about books was so like her.

I wasn't sure how long I would stay, but I would make sure that it would be taken care of before I left. I would hire someone to help me out and then train them to take over. In the end I would have her library in ship-shape before I left for England. For now I planned to mourn her.

I played with her mother's wedding ring as I took a stroll down the stairs and into the library. A storm was rolling in off the banks, and from the sound of the weather forecast, it was to be a nor'easter. I was already bundled up in my favorite sweatpants with my best robe. Shuffling my slippered feet across the library to Gram's desk, I turned on her overhead lamp and took a closer look at the ring. It was beautiful. I had admired it when I was a small girl, always touching the diamond in the center. It was what I envisioned my own wedding ring to look like when I grew up. It held a round diamond in the center surrounded by platinum. The band itself was a rose gold and etched into the sides were small leafy hearts. I slipped it onto my right ring finger and looked up and outside the window. The snow blew past them in huge tufts, and I saw the windows were starting to frost over. It was all very creepy being in the library alone in this weather. I needed a book and to cozy up in my bed upstairs. I stood up and as I did the power went out.

"Shit!" I squeaked.

I hated being alone in the dark. I fumbled around on Gram's desk searching for her flashlight. I hit it with my hand as it rolled across the desk and landed with a thud onto the floor.

"Double shit!"

I bent down on my hands and knees and felt along the floor hoping not to touch anything gross. My hands grazed something odd. I felt along its edges. It was hard and didn't seem to belong there. Now my curiosity had me crouching in the dark trying to figure out what this was. Finally I found the flashlight and clicked it on. Focusing the light, I saw the odd thing sticking up like a broken piano key. It was a floorboard upended. I pushed it to get it back into place, but all that did was make it fly up further and then completely out of the floor.

"Well, that's just great," I told myself.

I was here in the dark talking to myself. I dared to take a look into the floor, hoping not to find a rat family living inside or a web housing a large spider. I did find something, but it wasn't sinister; it was a set of books in a case covered in plastic wrap. Reaching in, I pulled them out. The dust on it was at least three inches thick. This must be the special book collection Gram told me to read and to keep safe. Anything that was precious to her, she hid—like the money I found pinned to her clothing in her closet, or the other jewelry she had taped to the back of her dresser.

I brushed the dust off and opened the plastic to find four books inside. They were pretty good in size and looked to be in great condition. They didn't have traditional covers that you'd see in a bookstore. Instead they were covered in a thick material to keep the books clean and the binding solid. I pulled the first book from the case and placed the others back into the hole. Covering it back with the loose board was easier than taking it out. I held the book close, and instead of going upstairs I went to my book nook. I had just washed the blankets the day before. Cozied up in the nook, I stared out the window one last time before opening the book. I decided I would only read for a little while before going up to bed. Gram *did* want me to read them after all.

I opened the first page to the title page; it was blank. I flipped the page and snuggled deeper into the blankets preparing to read the first chapter and that's when things changed.

Five

I blinked my eyes, trying to focus, and blinked again. I could see a floor and that I was lying on it. My face was smashed into it, along with bread crumbs, and I wasn't sure, but I thought I saw rat poop. I sat up slowly trying to get my surroundings figured out. It was hot wherever I was. Actually boiling hot, like a kitchen. I looked up and realized I *was* inside a kitchen, just not one I was familiar with. I'd never seen this one before and wondered how the hell I had gotten here. Standing up, I brushed myself off and came face to face with a stout old woman with her hair in a loose bun. She looked at me in surprise and instantly shrieked, "Where did you come from, eh?"

"Uh ..." I wasn't sure what to tell her. "I'm not sure. Can you tell me where I am?"

She placed her hands on her hips and duly wiped them on her apron that looked to me like it had seen better days.

"Where you are? Are you dumb, girl? Did you wander in here looking for a place to lay your head?"

I shook my head and said, "Me? No, I have a place to be and it's not here. I just need you to tell me where I am, and

I'll get out of your hair."

I looked around the kitchen, noticing the giant pots of soup on the stove. She was running this kitchen, that was clear, because she wasn't alone. In another room a whole slew of workers ran around, so busy that that they didn't notice me. I peered outside the open back door and saw a green hillside with lush grass and trees. It was daytime, the storm was over, and it was actually hot enough outside to have the doors open. I walked toward the door and got a closer look.

"This isn't Maine," I whispered to myself. There were nothing but hills as far as the eye could see, and it was hot. Maine this time of the year was nothing close to hot. It was freezing cold.

"Maine, did you say?" the cook asked.

"Yes, Maine, as in the state. Where. Are. We?" I was losing my patience with this old bitty, and I needed answers.

"I have half a mind to grab my broom and whip you with it, lass. Don't ya talk to me like I'm dull. You're in my kitchen, remember?" She had an accent. She sounded either Irish or Scottish. She sure as hell wasn't a Mainer.

"I'm sorry, I didn't mean to offend you. That was rude of me. I'm just really confused."

I placed my hands on my head as it spun. I really was sorry, but this wasn't right. Where I was standing wasn't where I was supposed to be.

"Are you from the Americas?"

The Americas? What kind of question was that?

"Yes, I'm from America." I wondered why she referred to it as the Americas, but I didn't dwell on it, there were stranger things at stake here. "I'm Emme."

"I'm Nancy, and I'll tell ya that ya need to be leavin' before the master gets back from his ride. If he catches you in here with me, you're in for it."

"The master, who is he?" I asked, backing up a step. The heat from the kitchens and the threat of this master made my hands shake.

"You really are daft. Do you know whose home you're in? And look at ya. What in God's name are ya wearin'," she asked as she touched my robe. "What is this frock?"

"I beg your pardon, *Nancy*, this is a nice terry cloth robe from Dillard's." I looked down at it and then nodded. "You're right, it's terrible. I just need a phone. I'll call my friend to come get me, and you can go back to cooking."

Rose wouldn't be happy having to drive here, wherever we were, but she'd do it. She was a faithful friend.

Her eyes widened and she shrugged. "A phone? What is that? Some fancy American tool, it must be."

Oh. My. God. I've died and gone to hell. I'm gonna be stuck in a kitchen with Nancy for all of eternity and there are no cell phones. Did I die in the library? I quickly thought back to the last thing I remembered: reading in my nook while a storm blew around outside.

Nancy grabbed my hand suddenly and inspected my ring. "Where did you get tha'?"

I yanked my hand back and held it close to me. "My Gram gave it to me, why?"

Nancy seemed to also have an eye for beauty, but she better keep her grimy cook hands off Gram's ring.

"I know who ya are, that's why. As I live and breathe, I never thought I'd see the day. Come with me child, up the stairs with ya."

I didn't argue; I just moved up the winding staircase to the upper half of the home. The heat gave way the higher we climbed, but I grew more concerned about where I was and where she was taking me. Nancy seemed to know who I was and that meant getting home, so I followed.

Now that I saw more of it, I could see the beauty in this home. Hardwood flooring that was probably original as were the windows panes because they had that old warping to them. But they were clean and looked amazing as the sun shone in. Nancy pushed me into a room where a small bed sat and a huge cabinet hung open. I glanced at some of the clothes that hung on the hangers. I saw a lot of lace and even more silk. Whoever lived here liked vintage clothes, that was for sure.

Nancy closed the door behind us and a smile grew on her face as she inspected me.

"Where are ya from, lass?" she asked wide eyed. She'd become a nicer lady upstairs like a switch turned off.

"Maine. Well, I live in California now, but—"

"No lass, what *year*?"

I swallowed. Nancy was bonkers. Even crazier than Crazy Joe that lived down the block from me as a child. He used to talk to birds and telephone poles.

"Okay, this isn't funny anymore. Nancy, I need to get home. Can you help me with that?"

She stopped smiling and at that moment grabbed my arm and squeezed.

"I'm tryin' to help ya. But I need to know *when* you're from."

The way she said *when* frightened me, and I'm not sure why.

I just told her, "2017."

I whispered it like it was a secret she should never tell anyone. As I did, her eyes widened and she whispered to me, "Well, dearie, you've landed yourself in 1892. And this home resides in Worcester, England. The master of this household is Jack Ridgewell. This party that I'm planning is a dinner for his going away. He leaves us for the Americas in precisely one week. It is there that he will be making settlement." She looked almost sad after she told me this.

"So, I'm in England, and I'm in a house where a party is going to happen any second? Oh, and no big deal but it's 1892, not 2017!"

She nodded and looked happy that somehow my daft self was following along with this madness. This was crazy. This was worse than falling down the rabbit hole. At least Alice was able to eat cake that shrunk her and meet talking animals. I was stuck with a crazy Scottish cook.

I looked around and saw this home and the way Nancy spoke and dressed; it was hard to disprove Nancy's words. If I tried to argue any other reason for landing in this house, I couldn't. I couldn't come up with any reason of why I was surrounded by the heat of summer when I was just in the dead of winter. Maybe I was dreaming and not dead? If this was just a dream, then I had to just go along with it until I woke up.

I wouldn't be stuck here forever. *Yay for that.*

Was this crazy? Of course it was. But what was I to do?

"How do you know of me?" I asked her.

"Ah. Your ring," she said, pointing to it. "I've seen it before. It was on the finger of a beautiful lady named Miss Grace Bailey. She was here in this house with Mr. Lockhart."

"But I don't understand. Grace Bailey was my great-grandmother," I said, my mouth going dry. How on earth could she have been here? The timeline and dates didn't add up. *Just a dream, don't forget that.*

"She was a lovely lass, and Mr. Lockhart explained how

they arrived to be here. It was all, of course, very confusing and hard for me to believe that they traveled here through a book."

"A book?" I asked her shaking my head. Books could take you places when you needed to escape, but to think that they actually helped you time-travel was pure madness.

"Yes, the strangest thing I ever did hear. I liked them plenty, so we had a party in their honor. Of course Mr. Ridgewell didn't know when they were from. He wouldn't understand tha'."

Maybe Nancy was a little more open to certain possibilities.

"Mr. Lockhart? Would that be Harold Lockhart?"

It had to be the same one. The scientist who owned the library before it was Gram's.

"Ah, yes. That's the one. Do you know him?" Her smile spread from ear to ear, and it was easy to see that Nancy liked him plenty.

I shook my head. "No, he's dead now. What year did they come from?"

I couldn't believe I was asking this question. Shit, I was merely playing along.

"1937, it was. The only reason I believed the man was because I saw them appear and then vanish before my very eyes. Truly amazing, that was."

In that year, my Gram would have been born three years after, and Grace would have been pretty young. I wondered how on earth she knew Harold Lockhart. Were they friends? I did know Harold died shortly after Gram bought the library from him. The thing about dreams was things never made sense to you while you dreamt them, and this certainly fit the bill.

"She traveled like you did. Harold told me that others would be coming someday, but I just didn't expect ya so soon after their visit." She ran a hand over her graying hair and smiled again at me. The mean woman that I saw downstairs disappeared. Nancy was just simply doing her job for her master. And I was staring at her in disbelief.

"He's been dead for many years, so it wasn't recent," I informed Nancy. "Do you know how they traveled here, what they did?"

She thought for a moment and said, "They used tha' ring and a book. I thought witchcraft at first, but no, Mr. Lockhart told me it was science and magic of the old."

I was so confused my head spun. How could Grace have been here by traveling through a book?

I sat back onto the bed and let my mind spin up crazy notions. Nancy opened the window and let the cool air blow in.

"Are ya all right?" she asked, concerned.

"No, not really, but I think I'll manage."

"We must get you dressed then. If it's anything like Grace's visit, you'll be with us for a bit. You must blend in. I can't go hiding you anywhere about the house."

"*Blend in*? Oh no. I don't see why I can't stay here until whatever spell I'm in wears off. Or I wake up from my nightmare." I nodded and smiled like a crazy woman.

"No. You can't hide. There will be guests arriving soon, and they'll be staying in all the rooms. The only room that won't be full of people is the basement. Trust me when I tell you, you don't want to hide in there too long." She chuckled and a small laugh escaped me, although it wasn't funny. Not even a little.

She was busy looking for clothes in the closet as I stared

out the window. Just how long would I be staying here? What would happen to my life back home?

Maybe I was in a coma at home and Rose was busy trying to find a cure for me. I thought back to time-travelling movies I had seen and it hit me. Gram wanted me to read the books. She was adamant about it. She called the library magic and said that only *I* could read the books. The book sent me here, so maybe the me in 2017 was still at home nestled in the reading nook. Maybe the storm was still going on outside as I was reading and was somehow transported here. Or perhaps I was sucked into the book itself and *that* me disappeared for a while. If that was so, then Grace and I were reading the same book. If she came here with Mr. Lockhart, then the book was somehow our transportation. And maybe it wasn't a dream at all. Maybe it was really happening.

I wondered how exactly Grace and I came to travel here, but all the who's, how's, and what's would have to wait because Nancy was pulling off my robe and swatting me.

"Off. Off. Put these on."

I put my hand up and stopped her. "I can take my own damn clothes off, woman." She looked at me like I had three heads. I undressed to my bra and panties.

"What on earth are those?" She asked pointing to my lacy red bra and panty set.

"This is from the finest undergarment store in the United States," I told her proudly.

"I don't care if God made it himself, it all comes off," she said as she shoved a complicated looking garment my way. "This goes on and I'll lace you up. Can't have you wearing contraptions like that for undergarments. People will take notice."

"What does it matter what I wear underneath? I'm not

going to do a striptease. Am I?" I winked at Nancy, and she swatted me again.

I pulled up the item she placed on me to get a better look and upon inspection noticed it was a corset.

"How am I supposed to breathe in this?" I asked as she wrapped it around me. I held my breasts so she couldn't see them.

"No time for being shy." She shoved my hands away and tightened the corset. She heaved, and I held onto the wall for support. "All proper ladies wear corsets, not red undergarments."

She handed me what I think were supposed to be underwear, and I put them on like a pair of pants. They were baggy and comfortable like the sweatpants that Nancy made me take off. But I refused to take off my panties. What difference did it make if I wore them under what she made me put on?

She handed me a mauve dress that took my breath away. I held it up and tried stepping into it, but she stopped me.

"No. I'll do this part." She placed it over my head and it slipped down over my body.

"This is the finest dress from France and was meant for Miss Everly to wear, but she passed last month."

I was wearing a dead girl's future dress. *Great*.

"How did she die?" I asked as she laced up the back of the dress, which made everything tighter.

"Carriage accident. She was staying here for a while in hopes of a marriage engagement with Mr. Ridgewell, but he was too smart to marry a girl like her."

"Why do you say that?"

"Because she was stealing money from him, ordering dresses on his account, and she treated the staff terrible. If ya ask me, she was a snob." She pulled her nose up in the air, making me laugh. "Now look at you. You'll blend in just fine."

I looked in the oval mirror that stood in the corner of the room. I looked like I was from the era; I looked elegant.

"This is so strange," I said to myself. I pinched my skin and slowly raised my head to see my reflection in the mirror. I was still there. It wasn't a dream. It was so messed up though.

Would I ever go home? Would I have to wear corsets for the rest of my life?

I couldn't do it. I'd be a cook in a kitchen for the rest of my stay here or even sleep in the basement if I had to. But this damn corset wouldn't stay on this body. No way!

"Now," Nancy said pulling me away from the mirror. "You can go down the stairs and join the party. Just try not to speak to anyone, is that clear? You mustn't be noticed." She mumbled some more about hiding me away in the basement and then rolled her eyes.

I laughed. "Blend in, but don't talk to anyone. Sure, that'll be easy," I said sarcastically. This dress was not going to help me blend in at all.

"Nancy, when can you tell me about Grace being here? I need to know why I'm here."

She tsked and shoved a pair of kid gloves at me. I put them on and realized I liked the way they felt. "When I don't have a whole house full of people to cook for, that's when. Now, off with ya."

She practically threw me from the room and down the staircase. I made it to the bottom with her hot on my heels when she tore off into the kitchen. I wanted to follow her and to hide in the kitchen. I couldn't blend in. Who was I fooling? I wasn't elegant or well mannered. I was a mouthy nineteen-year-old who didn't care what people thought. I didn't speak properly for this time period. Sure, I'd seen old movies, but I didn't have the first clue how to dance or even what women in this time were allowed to say. I was suddenly missing my time period so much that the thought of being stuck here almost brought tears to my eyes. I wanted nothing more than to be back at Gram's house and out of this stiff dress.

I hesitantly peered around a corner and heard music being lightly played in a small room to my left. It sounded like a piano and a harp possibly, but I didn't know much about music. Again, I missed my time. Not in the mood for chatting with anyone, I just wanted to get the hell out of here. Surveying the rooms, I tried to find an exit that would allow me entry to get back home, but to my dismay there was no door marked *Here to 2017*, anywhere. So I was screwed. I hurried across the hallway and entered a large empty room.

It seemed like a nice enough room to hide in, but there was no exit. There was a window, and for a moment I considered climbing out of it and running to the town, but what would I do once I got there. No cell phones. Hell, no phones at all. I was stuck here until God-knows-when.

I stared out the window at a man and woman. They were walking the grounds; her hand was placed slightly on his arm. It was so strange being here. If I wasn't seeing other people walking around, I'd be sure I was going nuts. But other people were here, and that meant that I wasn't delusional; I was really here. This wasn't a dream at all.

Somehow I was really in this time period, and I made up my mind as I looked out at the grounds that when I got home, I'd find out how it happened. I'd make sure it never happened again.

"Ahem," a loud cough startled me from behind.

I turned and faced the man from which it came. He was

tall and had a strong sturdy frame that I noticed filled out his shirt and jacket well. His light brown hair had a slight curl to it that hung low on his forehead. His arms were crossed and ankles as well as he leaned against the archway that led into the room. He looked casual as he pretty much checked me out from top to bottom. His stern face broke into the most adorable, heart-stopping smile I have ever seen.

"I don't think I've had the pleasure of an introduction," he said in a British accent that made me start perspiring in a good way.

"Uh..." I paused. "I'm Emme."

I went to stretch my hand to shake his, but when he didn't reciprocate I pulled back casually.

"Emme? That's an unusual name. Is that a family name?" His lips were full and kissable, and I couldn't stop staring. With that accent and those lips, he was lucky I didn't attack him right then and there. He was the epitome of hotness in a late twentieth century kind of way.

"No."

I couldn't think or speak around him, it was pathetic. It must be the corset.

"Well. Is it just Emme then?"

"Emmeline Bailey," I answered quietly. What the hell was wrong with me?

All of a sudden I was a drooly shy mess. This was not like me at all. Where was my confidence and bold behavior?

He laughed slightly and then said, "Emmeline is a name far too beautiful to be ignored. As are you. Why are you in here alone, Miss Bailey? You have no escort with you?" He looked around, and when he found no man in here with me, he looked almost worried for my safety.

My heart skipped a beat. "I'm new here?"

Pathetic. Just pathetic.

"Then we shall change that right away." He smirked. I think I could have swooned at that moment, but I held myself together.

He took my hand and kissed the top of it ever so slightly. I could have sworn I felt heat burn its way through the gloves.

He let my hand go, but I longed for him to keep his lips there all day. I didn't know men in this time period looked this hot, but he was living proof. He wore a double breasted coat that was short in the front and long in the back. It was brown velvet and looked amazing with his blue-green eyes and brown hair.

His pants were of the same material, and on his feet were high boots that looked ready for a horse ride. I suddenly wanted to take all of his clothes off. It was the most indecent thought for the moment and my cheeks heated. Here he was being polite and I was thinking about undressing him.

His hand came to my cheek and he ran his fingers across it. "Are you feeling all right?"

I blushed even more from embarrassment and nodded. "It's hot in here."

I had to come up with something.

"Well then, we shall walk the courtyard until you're feeling well," he suggested, as he extended his arm. "I'd love to hear all about where you're from. And since your escort seemed to wander off, I shall take over that duty today."

I took his arm like I saw the girl do outside and he led the way. We went out into the cool air, and I could feel my cheeks go back to normal. The country was breathtaking. Green as far as the eye could see. I spotted a stable and horses and carriages. It was so strange not to see cars and a highway. I was struck with the thought of how the city and this home looked in in my time period. I was sure it didn't look like this anymore.

That saddened me. Things were so much simpler here, and I wished they would have stayed this way. It made me think of all the changes they were trying to make in Bay Ridge while I was away at college.

"Are you feeling better, Emmeline?"

The way he said my name was thrilling, although I usually hated it. From a very young age I had asked to be just Emme, instead of Emmeline. I thought Emmeline was an old lady name and wished my parents could have named me something normal.

Coming from his lips though, I gained an appreciation for it. He smiled at me and a dimple formed in his cheek that matched the one in his chin. God, he was perfect. Why was he walking me around the courtyard? Why not some beautiful English girl?

"I feel better, thank you." I decided to speak in short sentences so he wouldn't notice I was talking so oddly while trying to get to know him at the same time. "You never told me *your* name."

"We have plenty of time for that, don't we? I mean to get to know you first, Emmeline."

"Ah, you're being mysterious then. Okay, I can play that game."

He laughed and squeezed my hand. His laugh was melodious, and it made me giggle a little. I'd actually met a perfect specimen, and I didn't even know his name.

"Where are you from, Miss Bailey?"

Oh, I'm from the future. No big deal. I parked my DeLorean in your stable.

"I'm from Maine, and you can call me Emmeline if you

want. I actually like the way you say it."

We stopped walking and he smiled even bigger than before.

"You're from Maine? That's wonderful. Surely you can fill me in on everything I will need to know. I've been trying my best to learn the language."

Learn the language?

"I don't understand, are you going to Maine with Master Jack?"

He laughed, and his stunningly blue eyes twinkled as they hit the light.

"Yes, you can say that. I'm eager to arrive in America."

"It's not as beautiful as this, trust me."

He nodded like he understood, but he didn't. Once he arrived in America, it wouldn't be like this, not for long. Soon he would learn to miss his home as I had missed mine while away at college. But like me, he'd get used to the differences and learn to hide the disappointment. He laughed and before long, sadly, broke free from me.

"Your American language is much different from England. You say words I find hard to understand. Maybe you can assist me?"

Oh, I'd love to assist him, but what I had planned didn't involve talking.

"I can help you learn the lingo if you'd like. One condition," I teased.

"Anything," he said as he took my arm again.

"You teach me the ways of your time, ah, I mean world. And you tell me your name."

He nodded. "I'll do my very best." He placed his hand over his heart and said, "My name is—"

At that moment the valley started to get hazy and blurry;

I clung to him not sure what was happening. Then I heard my name being called somewhere in the distance, and that's when I was no longer looking at England or my handsome stranger but staring at Rose instead.

Six

"I've been trying to wake you up for at least five minutes! You're a deep sleeper," she exclaimed, as she sat down next to me on the bench. I was back in the library and in my hands was the book. So, it was just a dream then. I had in fact been asleep, and I was dreaming it all. England, time-travel, and my handsome stranger was all a fabrication of my sleeping mind.

What a dream to have, though. He was perfect!

I wanted nothing but to be back there with him. His voice was so real, and I swear I could still hear it as if I was there with him still.

"Sorry," I muttered.

I looked outside. The stormy night had passed, and day had appeared in its place. Snow covered the ground as plow trucks tried to work their way onto the heavily packed roads. No doubt there was a foot or more of ice under that snow, which would make for a messy few weeks. I wished I was back in California. They didn't have snow like we have here in Maine. I can't even recall one cold winter night there. I shivered just thinking about stepping outside in that mess.

"So," Rose said, breaking my train of thought, "what are you reading?"

She pointed to the book that was now closed and missing a page marker. I pulled the book up and for some reason hid it underneath a stack of children's books.

"Nothing really. Just a book on history," I lied.

I realized then that Gram asked me to protect the books and here I had it out in the open. To be honest, I didn't really even attain any information about the book itself; I must have fallen asleep before I got too invested.

"I came by to see how you're doing here all by yourself?" Rose asked, looking concerned. She was really good at that look. She had it down to a science it seemed.

I ran my fingers through my tangled hair and realized I needed a shower. Curly hair was terrible in the morning. There was never a good morning look when your once fresh bouncy curls were flattened all night long.

"I'm doing okay, I guess. Dealing with Gram's loss has been tough. The weather doesn't make it any easier." I pointed to the cold street and the dark morning sky. "I need to sort things out today, hire a librarian, and get back to school. But I made that stupid promise to Gram." I mentally kicked myself.

"It's okay to hire help, Emme. Maybe if she works out, you can get back to school. But transfer here first and take night classes until you figure it all out." It was actually an awesome idea to transfer. It wouldn't take me long to finish school and train someone to take over the library; I'd be in England in no time.

"I heard that this big company was trying to buy your Gram's library for millions of dollars. It could be worth hearing them out, ya know?"

I recalled seeing letters from some company on Gram's

desk. The thought of selling this place made me literally sick. What would they want to do with an old building like this, other than the land?

"Well, I have a shift," Rose said as she looked at her watch. "Call me later?"

"Yeah."

My mind was now on other things. I felt bad about blowing Rose off, but I was kind of scatterbrained. I hadn't returned her calls lately, but I would start being a better friend. I hugged her goodbye and got my butt in the shower.

As the hot water ran over my chilly skin, I couldn't help but think back on the dream I'd had. It all came back to me as if they were memories, but I knew that was crazy. Nancy the cook wasn't real and neither was the dreamy guy that I had met. I let the dream go and decided it was time to focus on real life.

After I conditioned my hair tremendously and ran my fingers through it a million times, I tackled the letters on Gram's kitchen table. Numerous bills, which to my surprise had been paid months in advance, and letters from the builders that wanted to take over the library. It was the same company as the one demolishing downtown Bay Ridge—JR Builders. I ignored the letters for a minute and looked at the bills one more time.

I couldn't figure out how Gram paid all these bills so early. I knew she had some income coming in, but I wasn't sure what the revenue was from the library. It was not a government owned library. She owned it all herself. She bought the books, computers, shelves, and more. She paid off the building herself, but taxes were taken every year. Also there were standard building expenses and living expenses. The big question was: how was I going to afford to keep the library open and running when I myself had no money?

I shuffled through the bills and set them aside for a moment, and laid my head down on the table.

"How am I going to do this, Gram?"

The phone rang and I reached up for it. "Hello," I mumbled into the receiver.

"Mrs. Bailey?" a man asked.

I sighed, "No. Mrs. Bailey passed away." I hated saying those words. They felt so awful on my tongue.

"Oh." He paused. "I'm so sorry to hear that. My name is Jason. I'm calling about a few letters we tried to send her a few months ago. I have been trying to get ahold of her for some time, but our paths never seemed to cross."

Letter?

Wait.

"Are you from JR Builders?" I asked now sitting up. I would be giving this guy a piece of my mind.

"Yes. I am—"

"What do you plan on doing to my Gram's property?" I interrupted.

"Well, I'm glad you asked. We think the property would be a fantastic place for a shopping plaza. A lot of people in town seemed like they would like to have a better location for a food market. Your town doesn't have much variety in way of clothes shopping either." He went on and on and I let him talk. Food market. Clothing stores.

Was he kidding me? The trees that surrounded the library would have to all be cut down. The building would be torn down and replaced by a shopping plaza. All the work that my Gram put into this place would be gone. All my memories would be torn down and turned to rubble for clothes.

"No," I said interrupting him.

He paused for a moment then said, "You haven't even seen the design sketches yet. They're amazing. And I promise you, once we talk, you will see my intentions are good."

I closed my eyes and willed myself to be strong.

"My grandmother wouldn't want her building torn down and turned into a shopping location for our residents. I mean, what good is shopping when the majority of the town is low income? This is a fishing village, not Beverly Hills. There is history in this town, and Gram would want it to stay that way. She made me promise."

"May I ask who you are?" His question threw me for a loop. Surely, he wanted to argue some more about my decision. Oh, I was really good at arguing.

"I'm the new owner of the library and the property. My name is Emme Bailey." I tried to sound grown up and dignified, like that would help in this case.

"Emme, my company is offering up a large amount of money for your grandmother's property. You said your town was low income, but building job opportunities could help create jobs. And in turn help the town create revenue."

He was right. It would create jobs for some of the families. It could potentially help the town, but I made a promise to Gram.

"Listen, dude, I made a promise not to sell. And you can talk your talk all day long, but the fact remains I'm not selling."

Hanging up the phone before he could argue his point any more than he already did, I was feeling weak and almost like I could sell to him. It was not my finest moment. I had to stay strong and keep the library up and running. I had to come up with an idea.

First order of business: hire a library assistant. Second,

figure out how to pay her.

I grabbed my old winter coat from my closet and zipped it up to my neck. Then came my snow pants, boots, and waterproof gloves. *Did I mention I hated winter in Maine?*

I trudged down the stairs to the door and wondered how on earth Gram did this every single winter. I mentally gave myself a pep-talk before heading out. I lived here before and I was used to the cold at some point, right?

As I opened the door, a wintery blast hit me in the face and I remembered why I had a ski mask in my dresser drawer. I salted the steps before I exited so I didn't slip on the ice. As I poured salt down, I couldn't help but wish I was back in my dream walking around in sunshine with the guy who had no name. It was warm there and everything about him was delicious. I mentally kicked myself back into reality and finished the steps.

My rental minivan was now gone thanks to Rose. She drove it to the nearest rental car place and turned it in for me. I now would drive Gram's old '81 Chevy around these rough Maine roads. I couldn't believe the thing still ran, but it did. It was a beast.

I hopped in and started the engine. The cold air made starting it on the first try a little difficult, but when it started, the truck roared to life. I drove down to the new coffee shop I saw on the first day I came back. I pulled into the parking lot and saw that I wasn't the only one in the mood for coffee today. Putting a coffee shop here was one of the smartest ideas this town had.

There were at least nine other people in line before me, and the one barista who looked disheveled at best. She took the orders then ran around like a crazed lunatic to make them. When it was my turn, I noticed her name tag read, Becca.

"Hi," she said, managing to sound bubbly. I felt bad for Becca and how frazzled she looked. Being nice to her seemed like the right thing to do. I also wanted my coffee made right.

"Hi. I'll take a house Cup of Joe with extra cream and an apple Danish, please." She smiled at my simple order and in a few minutes handed it to me.

"Thanks. Can I ask you a question?"

She looked back at her now empty line, took a breath, and said, "Sure. Ask me anything except for if we're hiring because my boss will say no."

I laughed and shook my head. "I don't need a job, thanks. Do you know the best place to advertise for a job position? *I'm* hiring."

Her dark brown eyes squinted as she looked at me from head to toe, no doubt wondering why someone so young was hiring for a job position.

"Are you from the city? Trying to hire people for the new construction?" She pointed across the street where JR Builders was now working hard to build a new shopping structure.

I laughed. "No. I'm hiring for the library. Mavis was my grandma."

She looked embarrassed as her cheeks filled with red. "I'm so sorry. I suffer from mouth diarrhea, and it hits at the worst possible moments."

I laughed. I liked her instantly.

"Did you want sugar in your coffee?" She pointed to my steaming cup.

"Nah, I like it without sugar." She poured herself a cup, and when I tried to hand her money for mine, she pushed it away.

"On the house. Sorry about my mouth, earlier," she said

again. "My little sister is looking for a job. She actually just moved back here."

"Oh yeah, from where?"

"College. It didn't work out for her." She put up air quotes and rolled her eyes.

"Ah, I see. Well, I'm trying to hire a library assistant so I can get the place running. I need to get back to school, but first I have to make sure the library is taken care of."

She nodded and took of her apron yelling, "Ma, I'm taking a break."

A woman with wild red hair, matching Becca's, stepped out from behind double doors and took over for her.

"Come sit, we'll talk some more," she offered.

It had been so long since I talked to anyone aside from Rose. So I followed her to a corner booth and slid in.

"Tell me about your sister."

She laughed. "Well, she needs a job. There's no doubt about that. She works hard, and she'll show up on time."

"Just not a college student then?"

She took a sip of her coffee and shook her head. "Nope. The first of us to get a college dream scholarship and she threw it down the drain. I could slap her silly. I mean, who does that?"

I knew a lot of people who entered school thinking it would be easy for them like high school was, but they soon learn it's a lot of work.. The studying and note taking, basically the learning itself, is all your responsibility. Most of those people do not do well in school. They'd flunk out or "take a year off."

I myself flourished in college. I never liked being told how to study in high school. I was, at times, way ahead of my professors when it came to work. As I sat with Becca, I realized I missed school and I missed my friends. I felt cheated when it came to my college experience since I only got one year in. I wanted to go back and to feel that fulfillment that I once had at Berkeley.

"I'll call my sister for you if you want. Her name is Tarryn."

I nodded and bit my lip. I tried to not think about my friends back at school and how I hadn't heard from them recently. I thought about how they'd love the girl sitting in front of me instantly, like I had.

The only time I did hear from them was to see if I was coming back. It was their loss, really.

"Yeah, see if she's interested. Tell her to meet me at the library tomorrow at ten," I said.

"Oh, crap. That might be a problem; she's looking at an apartment tomorrow."

I sipped my coffee and asked, "She doesn't have anywhere to stay?"

Becca shook her head. "No. My mom pretty much told us both after high school that we're on our own. We have to find our own way in life. I have my own place, but she can't keep living in my one bedroom."

Her mom seemed harsh to me, but I said nothing. Judging someone's parents wasn't my thing. I hadn't known my parents, and who was I to say that they wouldn't have made me do the same. Then a lightbulb went on inside my head.

"I can rent her a room if she wants."

"Really?"

"I have the space. Above the library is a full apartment, two bedrooms, two baths. And it's just me."

"Great. Then we'll see you tomorrow at ten." We drank

our coffee and I ate my Danish. Things were looking up so far.

Seven

The next morning before Becca and Tarryn arrived I cleaned the whole apartment. I moved my things to Gram's room and left my room pretty bare so Tarryn would have her own space to decorate as she pleased. I hoped she wanted to move in. I cleaned out my bathroom and set everything up in Gram's. Staring at her queen size bed, I suddenly wished she were lying in it watching Scooby Doo cartoons like we used to.

I pulled off her comforter and threw it in the wash. When it dried, I folded it neatly and put it up. I didn't feel right using her things. It felt better to put her things up for a while until I knew what to do with them. Her clothes all still hung in the closet and her toiletries still on the sink. I'd have to tackle those another day.

I sat down and emailed Harmony and Dawn to let them know I was still alive and well if they cared to know. I explained how hard losing Gram had been, how it still was. I let them know I wouldn't be returning to school, having decided to transfer to the online college program that the local college held. Call me lucky to find that they offered my courses I needed, and I could handle the course load until I was done. Although I didn't mention that their silence after finding out Gram died hurt my feelings and that I heard they already found another roommate on Facebook, what they did didn't matter anymore. I wasn't returning to that life and they knew it. I just needed to send this letter to tell them in my own words that I was moving on in my life, that I had no choice.

When I hit send, I heard a knock downstairs. I closed the laptop and ran down the stairs to meet the girls. Becca waved and said, "Good morning. I brought you a coffee."

I took the steaming hot cup while welcoming them in. "Boy, I'm sure glad I met you."

Tarryn was standing next to her wearing a nervous smile. She had a short blonde pixie cut with purple woven through it. Her nose was pierced and so was her lip. She was adorable and so punk rock that it made me smile. You didn't see many people like that here in Bay Ridge. It was nice to see it again. I got used to seeing diverse people in California. They were everywhere you looked.

"I'm Tarryn," she said.

"I'm Emme. Nice to meet you. Come on upstairs and check out the room and then we'll go over the library."

They followed me upstairs, and I showed them the room that would be hers and the rest of the apartment. They didn't talk much or ask many questions. When I was done, we went downstairs to the library.

"This is my Gram's library and it's pretty easy to run, but I'll need help filing books and helping at the desk while I'm running the children's story time. If someone needs help on the computer, you might have to help them," I told her. She nodded and played with her lip ring.

"Looks easy enough. I love books, and this is my dream job actually." It was the most she had said about herself yet. "How will it work out with pay and rent?"

That was the only part that I struggled with figuring out. Gram set aside money for me, and I had enough to pay her a salary and to pay myself as well for quite some time. It was like Gram knew I'd need help or that she was going to die. I tried not to think about the latter.

"The job pays minimum wage," I informed her. "It's five days a week: Monday through Friday. No weekends, so those are free to you. The hours are nine to five." I paused to make sure she was keeping up. "You'll have to buy your own food and cook it too. I'm not the best cook. Also if you could take a utility bill or two, I can take the others. I don't feel like charging rent is fair to you, but I need help with utilities."

A surprised look crossed Tarryn's face as she looked to her sister. "That's fair enough. Right, Becca?"

Becca thought it over for a minute, and I'll admit I was nervous. I needed Tarryn's help, and I didn't want to lose her because I sucked at running a business.

"Sounds good to me, Tarryn. You'll make enough to cover living expenses and have a little spending money left over. But, Emme, are you sure that's enough?"

I nodded my head and explained to her that I would be looking into government funding for the library soon. I had come across a website earlier before they had come that explained how to reach out to them for things like this. That seemed to make her more at ease.

The truth was once I saw that Tarryn was good enough at the job, I was leaving and moving to England. I didn't know Tarryn, but at this point I was desperate. If she did a good job and I taught her whatever I could, she could eventually run this place for me while I owned it. If anything went wrong, I was only a phone call away. It would still stay in my name, and maybe it could actually all work out.

"I want the job. I love the apartment. When can I move in?"

I laughed, "Whenever you want."

****

I spent the rest of the day filing paperwork for the funding process and preparing to open the library doors on Monday morning. I told Rose and Becca to spread the word. Tarryn had decided to move her smaller items in already, and she was asleep by nine the same night. It didn't seem strange to me that I had a roommate; instead it made me feel comfortable. I never lived alone before, and I would feel lonely otherwise. Tarryn was quiet, but I knew in time she'd get used to me and I'd get used to her. We just needed to get to know each other first.

Once I was done with the paperwork, I filed the books that were left on the shelf from when Gram was still here. As I placed the classic books on the correct shelves, I felt a longing to finish reading my mysterious book in my nook.

So, instead of going to bed at a decent hour, I climbed into my cozy space and picked the book back up. I didn't open it right away. Instead I inspected the outside for any sort of title. I found nothing of the sort. I flipped to the title page once more, trying to find my place, and that's when I saw the word on the page. It was just a simple "The" typed out on the once blank title page. I ran my finger across it and realized it was printed in ink as if the press had done it. I was sure the night before it was blank, but then again, I was sure my dream about being with a man was real. So I wasn't really a reliable source at the moment.

I found the spot where I ended with a dog-eared page. I absolutely hated doing this to the book and didn't remember it at all. I usually had a nice bookmark, but this seemed to be the only thing to mark the page before I had fallen asleep. Running my fingers across the crease at the corner of the page, I settled back and started reading.

I woke up once again facedown, this time I was in grass. I blinked my eyes and felt the blades of grass tickling my nose and lips. I pulled myself up and took a deep breath. I looked around and saw the fields upon which I had dreamt of the night before. I was back in England. I was dreaming the same dream. How odd.

There were times when I had thought I had the same dream over and over again, to only find out that it was my mind playing tricks on me. This was no mistake. I was, once again, in the same place.

"Emmeline, are you all right?" I looked up and blocked the sun from my eyes. The man from before was standing in front of me. "You...you disappeared. It happened so fast that I fear I cannot explain to you how it happened. Now you're here once again." He sounded really confused and, to put it lightly, so was I.

This dream felt way too real. It was exactly like before. So real and tangible that I couldn't explain it even if I tried.

"I...I don't know how I'm here again," I mumbled.

He reached out to steady me as I swayed to the side. "You've been gone for days. I worried I was going mad, that your presence was one of my imaginings. I dared not to speak a word to anyone about it. I have to admit, Emmeline, I've been going slightly crazed since I saw you last."

His hair was disheveled and he had grown a slight beard that only enhanced the sexiness of his strong jawline. His deep set blue-green eyes looked weary, and for that I felt awful.

My sudden disappearance had made him fall apart, that was apparent.

"I'll tell you, I feel like I'm going crazy too. Trust me," I admitted. "Can we sit somewhere? Out of the sun?"

"Of course."

He held my arm and led me to a tree in the center of the field. Once underneath the large tree, I felt instantly better. I looked down at my clothes and saw that I was, once again, in my own clothes. This time a little better than before. I was wearing yoga pants and an old T-shirt.

"I can't explain how or why I'm here. Hell, I don't even know your name, but I'm here again and I'm beginning to think that this isn't a dream. That I'm really here, with you," I said as I touched his arm. "I'm not from...here."

I didn't know how to explain it to him, but I did the best any girl who was somehow traveling through time could. I didn't have answers or explanations, but I had a gut feeling.

"I'm from a different time as you. As you can tell by my lovely clothing, I'm not from 1893."

He placed his fingers on my lips, stopping me, while shaking his head.

"This isn't right, Emmeline. Trickery at a time like this isn't fair," he said as he stood up fast. "I am leaving soon. I shall not have you doing this to me."

My mouth fell open in shock and I stood. "Do something to *you*? Listen here, buddy, I didn't ask for this. I sat down to read a book and then *boom*, I'm stuck in England with a stranger."

I pointed at myself. "Look at me. Do I really look like I belong here?"

He looked at my clothing and up to my hair, and I could see his cheeks redden.

"You are dressed very indecent, I suppose. No woman I've ever met wears trousers. Nor do they wear clothing that *fitting*."

I laughed. He thought *this* was indecent, he should see some of the dresses I had worn to parties. They were nothing like the dresses he was used to seeing on a woman. We absolutely didn't dress ladylike anymore. My sexy little black dress that currently hung in my closet would definitely shock some of the people of this era for sure.

"I don't know why I'm here. I'm absolutely not trying to, I don't know, hurt you or anything. I don't know how to go home." I slumped back against the tree. "I wish that I could prove to you that I'm not lying to you, but I cannot. You'll have to just believe me, I guess." It was as simple as that. He could either believe this bat-shit crazy explanation or not. One way or another, I didn't care. I just wanted to go home.

"I don't know why, Emmeline, but I feel as if I should say that I do believe you." He ran a hand through his thick hair, mussing it up. "I just don't know how else to explain your abrupt presence. One minute you are here and the next you're disappearing into thin air. I read many books on fiction, so I *suppose* it could be true."

"Well, I may know someone who knows something. She works for the lucky bastard that owns that house," I told him pointing to the house where Nancy was the last time I saw her. She was probably cooking something again for her master.

He smiled. "That house?"

"Yes. Her name is Nancy."

"Ah. Nancy. And who is this Nancy woman you speak of?" He continued to smile as if this was a joke, but I ignored it.

"She's a cook. I met her on my last visit here," I explained. "She's not the nicest person I've ever met, but I think she has some answers."

"I must argue that Miss Nancy is more than a cook. She's also the lady upon with which I trust my household while I'm gone. She's more of an aunt than a housekeeper," he said as he took my hand in his. "It's very nice to finally introduce myself to you, Emmeline Bailey. I'm Jack Ridgewell or you may just call me the lucky bastard."

Eight

We **walked up to the** grand house, and I couldn't help but feel like a complete ass. He was Jack Ridgewell, of course he was. Sure my life needed more complications, and I needed to deal with a young rich guy who thought I was making him go crazy. We'll just pile that on top of all of the other crap I had to deal with. And we'll throw in the fact that he's drop dead gorgeous as well.

He led me up the staircase that took us to the front of the house where a very burly man held the door open for the both of us. Sure enough, I smelled something cooking, and it smelled divine. Burly Guy closed the door and hung up Jack's hat and coat on a small hook behind the door.

"If you'd follow me, please," he said as he walked into the kitchen.

"Who's that?" I asked Jack.

"The doorman, of course. His name is Thornesmith."

Oh, the doorman. Duh.

As we walked, I noticed plenty of other workers tidying up the place or ordering them around. It was like watching Downton Abbey. I realized then just how rich Jack was. My hands began to sweat, and I ran them through my frizzy hair to try to tame it. The English weather was doing me no favors. I could feel my hair grow like it was a weed. It had a mind of its own.

"Miss Nancy, you remember our guest, don't you?" He pointed to me, and Nancy's eyes grew wide. She dropped her ladle on the stone floor and gasped. A young girl picked it up for her and Nancy didn't even notice.

"This isn't possible. How are ya here once again, lass?"

"That's what we came to ask you," I told her simply. "You knew about my great-grandmother and Mr. Lockhart. So it only makes sense that you'd know *why* I keep coming here."

As I spoke, she waved her hands wildly and shook her head.

"No. I'm not going to get involved in such a mess. I told ya the last time, I only met them that one time. Then they left for good. It was a while ago now. Jack was very young then."

"Miss Nancy, you must know something more. I beg of you," Jack pleaded. "You knew I wasn't well and you hid this from me all while watching me go insane."

His eyes looked so sad. He had a point. If he thought he was going crazy, then she should have told him. His puppy dog look did a number on her, and I found even myself feeling sorrow for the man. He was good.

She gave me a pointed look and said, "I told you not to speak to anyone! Now look what you've gone and done."

"It's not my fault. *He* spoke to me."

She looked to Jack and patted his face. "I hated to see you in such pain, but I couldn't tell ya. I was hoping you'd go to America and forget all about it. I never dreamed she'd be back."

I should have felt awful that he was going nuts here, but

I actually thought it was adorable that he thought about me.

I do admit I thought about him more often than I wanted to. But I thought it was just a dream—a beautiful one.

Thinking back on what Nancy told me about meeting Mr. Lockhart, I remembered that she said he said he combined *science and the magic of old* to travel here. So Gram was right, magic was real and it existed in these books. That was explanation enough for how they arrived and how I got here. But the whys weren't known yet. What made them travel here and why this time period?

I sighed and leaned against the wall, feeling the effects of the heated kitchen and the day outside drain me. I would never get used to living in this year, not without air conditioning. All I could do was hope this was a short trip.

"Are you ill, Emmeline?" Jack asked coming toward me.

"I'm just really hot. I'm not used to the weather. It's cold where I'm from, and I think it's getting to me." I plucked my clothes away from my body and suddenly wished for a small bikini. Anything would be better than what I was wearing.

Jack took me by the hand and led me through the door and out of the kitchen with Nancy following. We came to a small sitting room and Nancy opened the windows. A gust of wind blew in through the small window and I felt better. I could still use some air conditioning in this house though. What the hell did people do in this heat, besides die?

"The air is better in this room. You'll see that you will cool off faster," he said. "Nancy, sit!"

His voice was calmer but firm. Nancy knew something and she was hiding it. If he didn't get her to talk, I was pretty sure I could make her. I cracked my knuckles and settled my eyes on her. I tried for the tough chick look; I'm sure it did no good. With my frizzy hair and sweaty head, Nancy probably saw a train wreck of a girl in front of her.

She sat and played with her apron. "I remember that they told me the pages of the book were special. Mr. Lockhart was working on time-travel. Such a notion is ridiculous but nonetheless true."

I leaned forward and asked, "Did he say anything about the book itself? Why the pages are special?"

She shook her head.

"I'm sorry, lass. Just that he was trying to make history and Grace was the only one who could use the book. It was she that brought Mr. Lockhart. That's all I know. I swear it. May I go?"

"Yes. Ask Henrietta to bring Emmeline something to drink."

She shuffled off like a scared child while I leaned back against the uncomfortable chair.

"That makes no sense, but I'll deal with it when I get home. Lockhart might have some books in my library that will explain this."

It was the only thing I could think of. It wasn't like I could ask anyone to help me find answers. Everyone would think I was nuts.

"Your library?" Jack inquired.

I laughed at the fact that I had to explain this to people now. "I own a library. My Gram died and now it's mine. That is if I can get back to it."

"So you're a librarian then."

"I guess so. I'm also a college student. It's not what I want to be doing, but it's my life currently."

He nodded and I sensed that he felt the same. "Going to America isn't what I desire."

His expression turned serious.

"Why? What would you do if you could do anything?"

"I wouldn't be doing what my father wants of me. I would move to London and start my own trade company. But alas, I am my father's only son."

It was funny how things worked out in life. One minute you are living and dreaming of your future and the next you're living someone else's dream.

"We don't get to choose our lives like they tell us when we're little, do we?"

"No," he agreed. "We certainly do not. Being a child is much more innocent of a time and I often wish I was one again."

A young girl brought out a tea service and set it up at a table in the next room.

"Come, let's have tea. I'm not sure how much longer I'll have with you," Jack said as he walked into the room.

A smile crept upon my face at his words. He wanted to spend time with me, and the strange thing was, I wanted to be here. It made me forget about the library and my responsibilities.

He pulled out a chair for me as I sat as gracefully as I could in yoga pants. He smiled when I sat and shook his head.

"What?" I asked suddenly worried that I did something wrong or that I looked funny to him.

"Your clothing is shocking to me. I'm not sure if I'll get used to how different you dress." A blush ran across his cheeks.

Yep, I looked like a dork.

Great. Any guy back home would like my tight pants, but coming here, it's different.

"Next time I travel I'll make sure to dress more to your liking," I said smartly.

He held up a hand and his smile grew even wider. "No. Please. I'm trying to say that I enjoy your clothing. I like the way they look on you. I'd like to inspect the material if I could."

"You want me to take my clothes off?" I acted very offended, even though taunting him and making his blush grow wider was my real goal. "I thought the men in this era were supposed to be gentlemen."

"Emmeline, I do apologize. I didn't mean to say that I'd like to take them off myself...oh dear. I mean that when you take them off to change, can I inspect them? Oh bugger!"

He'd thrown his hands up in the air and went quiet.

"Jack, really it's okay. I get what you're saying. You've never seen material like this, right?"

"Precisely, I never intended to offend you in any way." He sighed with relief and ran his hand through his hair. He must do that when he's nervous because I had seen him do it before. I'd love to run my own fingers through his thick locks if he'd let me.

Jack had one of the most attractive faces I'd ever laid eyes on. It was one of those faces you saw only in movies and it made you wish you were born in another time period.

"I know that. I liked seeing you squirm. It was enjoyable," I said honestly. "In my time, men are very blunt. They'll tell you they want to take your clothes off with no hesitation. It's actually nice to see a man try to defend his virtue, is all."

He shook his head, all serious now, and poured my tea.

"Men are different in your time, that's for sure. It is very impolite to discuss matter of dress with a lady, and I'm sorry that I did. Yet, something tells me that I was the one who was more embarrassed. Am I right?"

I nodded. "It's no big deal to me. I'm used to it."

He stopped pouring and looked up at me sadly. "You're used to men being demeaning?"

"Well, when you put it that way, I guess the answer is yes."

He sat the tea down and gave me sugar and cream and stirred my drink. When he was done, I picked it up.

"That makes me sad to hear, Emmeline. May I speak frankly?" I sipped my tea and nodded once more. "You deserve a true and honest gentleman, for you may be the most beautiful woman I have ever laid eyes upon."

Now I was blushing furiously. A fire took hold of my face and I hid behind my teacup. No one had ever called me beautiful besides my Gram or maybe even my parents. Not my friends and especially not men. When a man saw me, he saw a conquest, and when I saw a man, I challenged them and showed them that I too didn't want anything but a good time.

Was Jack right? Did I deserve more from a man? If so, who in the hell would I find in my world to treat me like that?

"Why would you say that? Look at me, I'm in my Yoga pants and a T-shirt and I'm sipping tea in your gorgeous home. I'm not beautiful, I'm plain." I was defensive now. This was not the best reaction.

He took my hand as I set down my cup. "Please, never say you are anything but extraordinary. Why do you think I spoke to you when you first came? Because you blended into the background? No, because, Emmeline, you stand out."

What the hell was going on here? Was he actually flirting with me? God knows I wanted him to flirt with me. He was everything I looked for in a guy, but ten times better. Jack wasn't your typical guy; he was the guy who rode the white horse and became your gallant knight in shining armor. Except there was one problem, he lived in a book. He was a book boyfriend!

I wasn't even sure if he was an actual living human being. I saw him breathe and eat and drink, but was he real solely in the book? I couldn't help but want to ask him all these questions. I really wanted to know how it felt to be a book character, but then again as I sat here with him, I guess I became one myself. And maybe a character didn't know that they weren't real. They lived their lives as the author wrote it out.

The more I thought about it, the stranger it became. Was he fiction or not? I had to know the truth, but for now, I would bask in the delight he gave me.

"Are you embarrassed?" he asked, pulling me out of my trance.

"No. I think I'm shocked. No one has ever said that to me," I admitted.

"Would you like to see the rest of the house?"

Jack had changed the subject before things got awkward, thankfully.

"I'd really like to, yes. I don't think the hot tea was such a good idea. I'm even hotter now than I was before." I stood, and he took my hand and wrapped it in his arm. He felt warm, but a good warm.

He led me through the rest of the downstairs showing me a huge parlor and eventually we made our way upstairs. The tapestries that hung around the wall were astounding; everything in this house was like that. It was an honest-to-God mansion, and I was in it walking around and breathing it all in. It was the most beautiful place I had ever been, and I was in it with Jack. I felt giddy suddenly, and I had to fight to push the feelings back down.

"I've seen this room," I admitted when we passed by the

room I changed in.

"Ah. I was going to show you the library, not the guest bedroom."

We walked through the hall and into a library that was nothing I expected: wall to wall books from floor to ceiling. In the corner a large fire place that thankfully was not lit. The other corner held a door that led out to a small balcony.

"It's beautiful, Jack."

"I thought you'd enjoy it. Yet, you did say you didn't like being a librarian, so we do not have to stay in this boring old room."

"No! No, please. I like it here," I admitted. He laughed softly to himself.

"The girl who wishes a different career for herself loves books after all. Hmm."

He was teasing me and I liked it. Letting my hand go, he sat in a large overstuffed chair.

"I enjoy it here as well. It helps me think."

I scanned the walls and the books and asked, "What do you think about?"

"Loads of things, really. Mostly how I can get out from under my father's thumb and start my company. Then I laugh to myself over such an idiotic notion."

I stopped and looked at Jack. "You can do anything you want. You're a grown man, aren't you?"

"Why yes. I'm twenty. Emmeline, it isn't easy for a man my age. I simply cannot break free like that. I'd lose his support and his trust. And a man like my father has many allies and a man cannot defy his father."

He'd lose his money, and for a man in this time, money and status was everything. I got it, I really did. Money and status were important in my time, too.

"You know, everything we talk about defines us by our time periods we live in." I pulled a book from the shelf and inspected the cover. "We aren't simply just a man and a woman right now. We're 'Jack's World' and 'Emme's World.' The things we speak about won't be the same. I won't be able to help you get through what you're going through because I simply won't understand. Things in my world are so much different. They aren't that complicated."

He bit his thumb and looked incredibly sexy while doing it.

"So, if they aren't so complicated, why are you a librarian instead of at finishing school?"

Damn it. He had me there. I turned and faced him, fully aware that I had no answer for him. The room started to spin suddenly and the colors of the books swirled together.

"Oh no!" I said as Jack stood and tried to catch me, but I fell too fast out of his world and back into mine.

Nine

This time I ended up waking—if you'll call it that—alone. No one was tugging on me and asking questions. It was just me and the book alone in the library. Tarryn was still asleep upstairs from what I could tell. I looked outside and it was still dark, so that meant I couldn't have been there too long. I hadn't been missing from this world for as long as the time before. Yet it was hard to tell where my actual body went while I was in the book and how long I was away. I really knew nothing. It was all just guesses and estimations right now. I needed to set up a video camera next time. I needed actual proof.

I pulled the blanket off my sweaty legs and opened the window a crack to cool off. My body was still heated; I could feel the weather lingering from Jack's world. I ran my hand through my hair and found it as poofy as it was when I was with him.

Him.

I actually felt awful for leaving again. Did I miss him? I wasn't sure.

I wasn't sure what I felt about anything that happened

to me or how I felt about this whole situation, but one thing was certain, I wanted to go back soon. I realized I wasn't any closer to figuring out why my great-grandmother was there.

I got up and scrambled to bed, exhausted from my little visit. I fell into bed still in the same clothes and looked forward to a new day where I could hopefully find answers.

The next morning I awoke to the sound of Tarryn cooking. I heard a lot of clinking and dishes being moved around. I pulled on a robe and shuffled into the kitchen. She took one look at me and handed me a cup full of coffee.

"You look like you need this more than me right now," she laughed lightly. "I made bacon and eggs."

She sat down a plate full of greasy bacon and scrambled eggs. "Thank you, Tarryn. But you don't have to cook for me in the morning."

"I know that. I *wanted* to. I like to cook, so I have no problem making meals for you if you're around." She smiled and dug into her breakfast. I did the same. Having her here wouldn't be so bad. We got along and she cooked, so that was a bonus.

In California, it took me a while to warm up to all of my roommates in college. Harmony and I hit a few rough patches in the beginning and we worked through it. Maybe living with Tarryn would be easier somehow.

"I have some errands to run, but I'll be back later to help you with anything in the library," she said as she finished her eggs.

I ate and nodded, saying, "I appreciate it. But we open tomorrow, so let's take the day off today."

"Sounds good to me," she said as she got up and rinsed her plate. "Okay, see you later."

"Bye. Thanks for breakfast," I told her as she walked out the door.

****

 Later in the day I found myself surrounded by college papers. I already had a paper due by next week, and I had just started the online class. This was going to be challenging for sure, but I loved it.

I reached for my cup of coffee and realized it was empty. This was no good. I sat up to stretch my legs and wake myself up somehow. I was down in the library's open space doing my work in the quiet surroundings. Gram had this room done for students who needed a little quiet time to do homework. How ironic that I was using it in an empty library.

I walked to the office where Gram did everything behind the scenes: ordered books, planned meetings, paid bills, and everything else a librarian does. The space wasn't very big, but it was big enough for Gram. I ran my hand over the small desk she sat in and realized that I remembered her working in here for hours sometimes. And this room was always off limits to me or Rose. We were never allowed in here at any time.

"What were you hiding, Gram?" I asked aloud.

I looked through the cabinets, now extremely curious about what she was doing in here all the time.

I found nothing.

So I went through her desk, still nothing. No clues left that I could see and no answers about why she needed me to guard this forsaken library.

I sat in her chair with a loud thump and rolled around the room. If she saw me now, she'd kill me. I pushed off the desk and the chair hit the wall behind me with a thud. I laughed then spun in the chair and rested my feet on the wall.

"Gram, why am I here? What the hell do you want from me, huh?" Tears now took over and the laughter ceased. "Why am I traveling into a book? Why does it have to be me? It's absolute torture to meet him and to be taken away so suddenly, especially when I'm so damn lonely without you."

Frustrated now, I gave the wall a good solid kick with both feet and the chair spun across the room. I looked up and heard a loud creaking noise.

"Oh shit."

I'd broken the stupid old building. The wall seemed to move slightly and I shot up out of my chair fearful of collapse. I stood there watching the wall shift and gradually, before my eyes, open. I gasped and looked into a room that was now visible in front of me.

A trick wall in my Gram's office. This was insane. I had once dreamt about Gram having a hidden room, but maybe it wasn't a dream. Maybe it was a memory,

It was like Narnia, and I was a kid again with hidden passages and magic books. I was going batshit crazy, so I did the only thing a crazy woman could do; I looked around for my trusty flashlight I put on the desk. I clicked it on and shined it into the large space. Dust and debris fell from the opening and I hesitated before entering. What would happen if I went in and the door closed? I'd be trapped because I didn't know the trick to opening it back up. I took a book and jammed it underneath the door for good measure before going inside.

The room wasn't as dark and scary as I anticipated it to be; it was actually quite the opposite. It looked like it had been in use not too long ago, a month maybe, before Gram died. It was a guess, but with this being her office, I only assumed she knew about this room. Books filled a small shelf on one wall and I found a hurricane lamp on a table. I lit it and its orange glow flooded the room. Posters hung on the wall with drawings of things I couldn't understand. From my best estimation they were scientific drawings full of numbers and calculations. Pictures filled up another wall. I noticed Gram in a few, but the others I had to really squint to see.

One photo held my attention. Four women in dresses, depicting the photo's origin were probably in Jack's time or earlier. I pulled the photo down and tried to see if any of the women looked familiar, but they didn't. One girl with dark curls resembled Gram from when she was younger, yet she looked different. A relative maybe.

I yanked the photo from the frame and found an inscription on the back: *The Librarians 1850.*

The fact that I'd been off about the year didn't even faze me. What did in fact shock me was the name they had for themselves. The Librarians.

Were they actual librarians, and if so, was this a family business? I wasn't so sure, but I would find out. I searched the wall for more photos of these ladies and found them. Some of them were with other people, but never were they all together again like they were in this one photo that I held in my hand. No, it could never be that simple. Not in my life at least.

The woman that looked like Gram was in a photo that read *1957,* and she looked exactly the same as she did in the group photo.

A curly-haired blonde was also in a picture from another date that read *1925,* and you guessed it, she looked the same. I needed to find out who these women were, so I took all the photos from their frames and flipped them over. I pulled out a sheet of notebook paper from a journal and wrote all the women's names and dates down. After a while I had everyone's name and the dates that they were in separate photos.

Jenny 1925, the curly-haired blonde.

Alice 1950, a feisty looking red head with a fierce smile.

Laura 1982, a pretty girl who looked shy.

And last but not least, Grace, my great-grandmother with her dark blonde curls. The same year, now that I remembered, that Nancy told me that Harold Lockhart and Grace arrived in the book. Things weren't making sense, but the pieces of the puzzle were lining up, if I could only fit them all together. I laid all of the pictures in a row and stared at them until my eyes watered. I had no answers, but I knew one thing; these women were together once and they were all from different time periods.

Did Harold find a way to travel through time? It was possible. It was also possible that the answers lie in one of the many books on the shelf behind me. As bad as I wanted to scour them and find out, I was dog tired and needed a break from this library.

I left the room and kept the door open, just in case. I locked Gram's office and headed upstairs. The house was still empty so I called Rose. She answered in hushed breath.

"Did I catch you sleeping?"

She sighed and said, "No. I'm at a guy's house."

"*A guy*? What guy would that be?" I teased. I'd caught her in the act of an indecent situation and I would revel in it. Rose was always the one who was shy about her relationships. She never talked about boys when we were young or sex when we got older. She was the modest one out of the both of us, but now I'd turned into a boring librarian. I hadn't been with a guy in months, and I decided Rose's love life was now a huge interest to me.

"Oh please, don't make this a big deal, Emme. I swear I'll kill you."

I laughed and said, "I swear I won't. Are you hiding in his house? Where is he?"

"I'm in the bathroom. I'm so embarrassed, Emme. I didn't mean for this to happen," she sighed. "He's only asked me out a thousand times, so I figured one date won't hurt, right? Well that date turned into...sex." She whispered sex like it was a dirty word.

"Good for you, Rose. You're turning into a little vixen; I like it."

"He's so hot, Emme. What the hell am I gonna do? We work together!"

I grabbed a cookie and munched on it while I thought about what I would do if I had been in her situation. I realized what I would have done was left the house right then and there. I wouldn't have considered the situation awkward at all. Being around him wouldn't have bothered me. But Rose, she was different.

"My best advice is to stay where you are and talk to him about it. He isn't married, right?"

"Oh God, no! What do you think I am?"

"Okay, calm down. I was just making sure," I said with a laugh. "Wait for him to wake up and have breakfast. Things don't have to be difficult or awkward. Relationships in the workplace work out all the time."

"That's really grown up advice. Thanks, Emme."

"Sometimes I can be a grown up. Now go back to bed and do something dirty with him," I half joked.

She laughed and said bye. I hung up the phone with a smile on my face. Good lord, I needed to leave this house. I grabbed my purse and my credit card; time for a shopping trip.

Ten

I nstead of going to the new stores, I went to the original shopping stores in town and splurged on a purse, new shoes, and a bunch of updated stuff for the house. I felt it needed some updated items in the kitchen and bathroom. There were paintings for my room and for the kitchen that I found. If I was going to live there, it needed some beauty. It wasn't exactly drab, but the '70s' style was killing me.

Becca was working at the coffee shop today, so I slid inside, avoiding a huge gust of wind and snow. I pulled my scarf off of my neck and hung it on the coatrack. Becca gave me a little wave and I smiled.

"Coffee and a Danish again?" she asked as she pulled her long hair up into a quick bun.

"Yes, please."

She made my coffee and, because it was dead, sat at a table with me. Hanging with Becca was easy. She was a very likable girl.

"So, what's the deal with the library?" she asked abruptly.

"Sorry?"

"Is it ready to go? Do you need help getting it ready?"

I smiled and set my cup down. "It's as ready as it's ever gonna be. I'm just not really thrilled that I have to take care of it. But a promise is a promise."

She shook her head and said, "That's admirable and all, but you have to live your own life too, Emme. What happens when you finish your schooling? Do you put off your dreams due to a promise?"

I shrugged. "I really don't know. I do know that I promised her that it would be me taking care of it."

Becca's family wasn't really close, not like I was with Gram. Her mom made her life hard, and she was the type of girl who ached to be free of this town and shake off her roots. I was like that too. Yet, now, I was stuck here again; although, I didn't long to leave like I had before.

"Do you have a boyfriend in California?" she asked, changing the subject.

"No. I had guy friends who were more than friends, if you could call it that. But I don't do the whole relationship thing."

She laughed. "What do you have against them?"

That was the thing. I had nothing negative to say about them, really. Relationships were good for some people, just not for me.

"I never wanted to be held down to someone. I would have to graduate and leave them, and I didn't want the complication."

"You just haven't met the right guy is all."

I pondered this for a moment. If I met the one, would I long to be with them all the time? Would it feel similar to what I was feeling for Jack?

I watched my parents' marriage as a child, and I had nothing bad to say about relationships when it came to my views. There were many happy people around me; I just never wanted to be one of those dependent women. I wanted to be able to travel and see the world. When I put my career in front of everything else, even family, I lost the only family I had. I wasn't around for the past year of her life. Had I known how sick she really was, I would have come home.

The truth was that when I looked back on my schooling, I felt sick. I felt regret for missing Gram's life and for not spending that time with her.

Getting close to someone would mean losing them eventually. And getting close to a man in a book meant I was going crazy. But the more I thought of him the more I longed to know him. The more I longed to do what I tried so hard to prevent in my life: let him in.

"Oh, no." I realized my mistake of saying it out loud and hoped Becca didn't catch it.

"What? Did you meet someone? You did didn't you?"

I shook my head hoping that she would give up and move on. But of course, she didn't. She pressed and pressed until I had no choice but to burst.

"I met a guy named Jack. It's really complicated." My hands clenched the coffee cup, and I hoped she would be satisfied with my answer. Of course she wasn't.

"Oh man. Tell me all about it. I live for hearing this stuff. I can't meet one decent guy in this town. I will live vicariously through you and Jack."

It was so true. This town held no wonderful catches except for if you were fishing out at the dock. The men here were in love with the sea, and they spent all their time with her.

"Who's Jack?" Tarryn asked as she came up to us and sat down. "A guy?"

Oh crap. I was in trouble now.

"Jack is an unattainable guy. It's not really even worth talking about, trust me." *Please leave it alone. Please, for the love of God.*

"What makes him unattainable? Is he married?"

Of course they weren't going to let it be, were they? No, because that was girls for you. Girls were catty and lived for gossip; trust me I am one. I used to live through my roommates' stories too. But there wasn't anything I could say to them that would make any sense. I couldn't tell them that I met a great guy in a book and couldn't wait to see him again. I'd lose them as friends, and I'm sure Tarryn would move out. No one needed to know my secret. It would be nice to tell someone. I wished I could spill about my travels to meet Jack and tell them about the book, but I had to stay quiet.

"He's not married. He lives far away. So it won't work out. You know, long distance and all," I said with a shrug.

"That's too bad. Not enough good men around here. Those that are, are already taken or moved away to a warmer climate. Like Florida," Becca said. "I'd love to just make a perfect man and plant him right here in Maine. I think I need to move."

I smiled. Becca deserved a nice guy. I wished I could find someone for her as I could see the loneliness in her from the first time I met her.

"We'll find you someone, Becca," I told her as I patted her hand. "How about you?"

Tarryn made a sour face and shook her head. "I'm good. I don't date. I don't have time for drama."

I heard that.

"Tarryn broke up with her ex, Fisher, last year. She had a ton of drama, that's for sure."

"Don't talk about me like I'm not in the room, Bec. Fisher's mom hated me. So it made the relationship hard."

She rolled her eyes and turned to me.

"Who could dislike you?" I asked seriously.

"I'm not your average girl. I like punk music, and I don't care for snooty adults who try to control their son's every mood. Let's just say I'm a mother's worst nightmare."

I could see that in Tarryn, not the nightmare part, but the part where she didn't like fake people. I could also see that she was delightful, funny, and caring. Any guy would be lucky to have her.

I had so much more work to do back at the library, so I excused myself from the coffee shop and headed back home. Tarryn and Becca had plans with their mom, and that gave me time to delve into the secret room and learn as much as I could about The Librarians' secret lair. In all honesty I did want to go back to Jack. But after talking to Tarryn and Becca, I wasn't sure if doing that was a good idea. I didn't want to grow attached to him. I needed to focus on my life here.

My grandmother's promise was tying me here, and I needed to cut the ties as soon as I could. If I kept seeing Jack, I wasn't sure if I would be able to stop. The fact was I was growing some sort of feelings for him. Feelings were bad. They never ended well.

Me and feelings did not mix well together. And that meant I had to stop traveling through the book for good.

Eleven

It was hard enough putting Jack's book back into the floorboards, but staying out of the library's secret lair was impossible. I had too many questions. Too many mysteries surrounded these Librarians. So that's why the night before the library re-opened, I spent my whole night inside the hidden room while Tarryn was out partying like an eighteen-year-old should.

I sipped a cup of tea and read as much as I could about these ladies. I learned more than any college could teach me about this subject, and my head hurt. I wasn't any closer to understanding *why* these women traveled through books, but I did know that they all did. They were a secret society of Librarians stationed all over the East Coast, and they traveled through books and time.

Yes. They traveled through time. In the past, not ever the future.

Their time was defined by books. Books written based on real people. So Jack was real, not fictional. Huge bonus for me and my sanity, but if he was real, that meant he was dead and gone by now. Long gone.

Each Librarian had a formula written that helped them travel. I'm not unconvinced that Harold Lockhart had tons to do with that. He was a scientist, and I know that he was with Grace when she traveled to Jack's time.

I wasn't sure how he could have helped them all, but if he could travel, that would mean he could go to their time period and help write the formula.

And there was another thing; all these women were my relatives. Yep. They were all my family. Family I'd never meet, but still, they were somehow related to my bloodline. They were Baileys.

Jenny Bailey. Alice Bailey-Carter. Laura Bailey.

Grace Bailey.

I put the teacup down and pulled the picture out of them all. I didn't see any resemblance, but there was one thing that pulled my eye to the photo. I pulled the light closer to make sure. I saw it there.

Each woman had a ring, brooch, or necklace that was the same as my great-grandmother's ring. Rose gold leaves surrounding a round cut diamond. Everything about it was exact, except for the way it was worn. That seemed to depend on the wearer.

Now, it was a ring. The same ring my great-grandmother Grace wore on her right hand.

I wished she were here now and that I could ask her who these women really were and what role they played. Why our family?

Why me?

"What are you doing up?"

I froze staring into Tarryn's eyes as she saw me in my grandma's secret room. I practically threw the photo that I held in my hand as I stumbled out of the room and tried to act casual, as if having a secret lair was totally normal.

Maybe for Batman.

But for me, it wasn't, and it showed as I tried to be cool, without really pulling it off.

"What's in that room?" Tarryn asked looking over my shoulder.

My cover was blown.

"Um, it's my Gram's room. It's where she holds her old photographs."

Smooth, Emme, like silk.

"Uh...why not just put them in the attic? That's where my mom puts them."

She knew something was up, but I couldn't make any more excuses for this room or for my secret. Maybe it would be nice if someone knew about this besides me. I could tell her everything, and she'd be okay with it. I decided how lame that was, and I grabbed her by the arm, gently, and shut out the lights.

"I think we should go out tonight to celebrate. What do you say?"

She struggled a little, but then relented. I knew I could get her to give up on that room with a night out.

"We'll go to Smitty's! I have a fake ID," she chimed in.

"That works perfect." My fake ID was still in my wallet, but I figured the staff there probably didn't even know who I was anymore. No one ever paid any attention to me anyhow.

It actually sounded horrible, but I needed to get Tarryn away from the library. And I could use a drink...or two.

****

Smitty's was packed with the usual suspects. Sailors

coming home after their full week or two of fishing or townspeople missing the sunshine. Our town was lonely at times, and the bars were the only place to go to have decent conversation. If you didn't own a computer, you were in Smitty's. Most people came here to drink and wallow in their self-pity.

I pulled Tarryn to the back of the bar and text Rose to meet us. Tarryn tried Becca, but she was stuck working still. I ordered a shot and gave it to Tarryn, who took it and downed it faster than I expected her to. I did the same to mine and ordered more.

Not shy about drinking, I could hold my own. I owe that talent to my year of college and sorority life.

There were many times that I woke up in the bathtub with puke in my hair, but those were the early days. The trick was to not mix hard liquor and beer or to drink hard liquor and frilly drinks. You started with a few shots and finished the night with something calmer, finally ending with a large glass of water and a pain killer. Worked for me every time.

We downed our second shots, and I ordered us Malibu and Cokes. Tarryn was beginning to loosen up and talk about what she liked to do when Rose walked in.

"Started without me, ladies?" Rose teased as she sat down. She pulled off her winter coat and hung it on the coat hook. "Still got that same fake, Emme?" I nodded and showed her my old ratty fake ID that I got senior year.

She wasn't wearing her scrubs, which meant she was off duty and not on call. Rose would never drink if she was.

"I'll have what their having," she told the bartender. "So ladies, what are we celebrating?"

"The opening of the library," Tarryn said holding up her drink. I did a quick introduction between Tarryn and Rose and left out the fact that Tarryn was underage, too.

Afterwards, I lifted my glass and toasted with them. I felt a foreboding within me. I wasn't celebrating; I was avoiding confrontation and trying to not think about Jack.

It was almost impossible not to think about him, especially when I watched people hooking up all around us. As the night went on, it got worse. I got more alcohol in me and I felt sadder.

"Rose," I started, "tell me about the guy."

Her eyes widened and she turned a bit red. Rose didn't like to kiss and tell, and I knew I was putting her on the spot. She didn't really date much either, which made her mother sad. If her family had the choice, they would have found a nice guy for her and married her off years ago. Her mother's Asian traditions didn't rub off on Rose. She wanted a career first like her father.

"He's a doctor at the hospital, and he's a little amazing. But I feel like we're keeping this huge secret from the staff. You know how much I hate that," she said to me.

I did indeed know that. Rose was honest and direct. She never kept anything from me or anyone really. It wasn't annoying but rather endearing.

"How did you get involved?" Tarryn asked.

Rose went into their story of how they met and I tried to listen, to give her my full attention. I couldn't help but think of my story with Jack. Jack was real, but he was gone now. If I tried to find him in my time, I'd find a grave. I took a drink of my Malibu and Coke and found the bottom. I was doing what I never did, letting a guy take over my thoughts. I was letting him into my high brick walls that surrounded my heart.

I never dated.

I never fell in love.

I absolutely never drank at a bar while thinking about a guy.

There were lots of times the girls in school would tease me and tell me I must be gay if I never had a boyfriend. What could I say? I never met the *one* who made my knees weak or made me want to commit. I had tons of friends who I would hang out with from time to time or go to school dances with, but never a commitment.

They all tried to make me their girlfriend; I think it was a challenge for most of them. Who would be the guy to make Emme Bailey fall head over heels for them? None of them would win that title, until now.

Of course, it was a guy in a book. A dead guy, who I had to time-travel to see. I put my drink down and leaned over toward the girls.

"I'm feeling a little tired. I'm gonna head back."

"I'll drive you," Tarryn said as she grabbed her purse.

I put my hand on hers. I needed to be alone and she didn't need to be driving.

"I'm going to walk," I said, giving her a reassuring smile. "I'll be okay. Just don't drink too much and do not drive. Our big day is tomorrow."

She gave me a sad smile, and I hugged Rose, who promised to come see me tomorrow at work. I nodded and grabbed my coat. I buttoned it tightly and braced for the cold breeze from the ocean. Once I hit the outside, it didn't come. The wind was absent from the cold night. I was thankful. The moon lit the street enough for me to see where I was going. I needed to be outside in the crisp air. I had to think of what I was going to do with my responsibility, of not only the library that Gram entrusted me with, but with the books. They truly were special, and I had to keep them safe.

I couldn't let anyone get to them.

I finally got to the library and unlocked the doors. Letters scattered across the floor from the mail. They must have fallen from my stack I carried in yesterday. I picked them up and absently walked, not to the apartment, but to the library.

I looked down at the letter in my hand and saw it was, once again, a letter from JR Builders. These guys were relentless. They wouldn't stop, would they?

I threw it in the trash and turned on the light above Gram's desk. I looked at the library and at all the books in each row. So many stories to be told and adventures to be had and an idea came across my mind.

Could I travel through them all if I tried? There was only one way to find out.

Twelve

I picked up the nearest book in the teen section and sat down in the nook; this time without my blanket. I looked at the front cover of the vampire novel that sent young girls into a tizzy, including myself. Who wouldn't want to be the apple of this vampire's eye? Who wouldn't want to be able to put themselves into the book and see him for real?

This was the true test to see if I could really travel into these books or if it was only the other books buried beneath the floorboards. Was it my family heritage that helped me with this talent or merely the library itself?

Gram did say the library was special. Time and time again she would tell anyone who would listen how important this building was; I just never paid any attention until now. Now, it was too late.

I opened the book, my heart pounding, and read the first line of the book. I read about a girl who was moving from her home in Arizona and nothing happened. I was feeling like this was all a waste of time and almost tossed the book down when I felt that familiar feeling.

I was standing in a forest of trees watching cars drive by

me and a girl, the girl from the book, driving with her dad to their home. I was inside this book!

I followed them as easily as walking, but I wasn't doing that. I was floating alongside them and as each word of the story was read, it played out in front of me more up close and personal than any movie could. I was really in it.

I watched as she met the vampire boy with the dark eyes and the fabulous hair. But there was such a difference this time; I could not talk to these characters. They didn't see me like Jack did. I realized that it was because this was a work of fiction. These characters, while they looked real to me, were not.

It didn't mean that I wasn't happy about being inside the book like this, but it was not the same.

I felt a pulling on my arm, and I looked around me as I stood once again in a beautiful forest full of trees. I looked around and saw nothing. But dang it, there was that pulling again.

Out of nowhere a hand reached through the trees and pulled me right out. I was sitting in my nook staring at Tarryn's worried face.

"What happened to you?" she asked, barely a whisper. "It was like you were asleep, but with your eyes open."

Her face was pale, and she looked terrified. I felt awful for scaring her like that, and I didn't do it intentionally. How could I explain what I was doing without sounding like a liar?

"I'm so sorry if I frightened you, Tarryn."

She shook her head and stood fast. Now anger was fully displayed on her face.

"You're hiding something from me; I know it."

I began fumbling for words. My mouth opened and closed like a dying fish, except I wasn't gasping for air, I was trying to find an excuse. Tarryn deserved more than lies and cover ups, but I couldn't give them to her right now. I didn't know anything myself. I had no idea how I could enter these books or what power I possessed that gave me this gift.

Dammit, Gram! How dare you do this to me?

How could Gram go all this year without me and never, not once, tell me about this? We lived in this library together and not once did it come up. Why did she wait until the last possible second to inform me about this rare gift?

"I can't tell you what happened because I don't know," I explained. "I found out that my Gram needed my help on her death bed, Tarryn. She made me promise to stay here because she said the library held magic. She gave me this ring and a whole speech." I told her as I held up my finger to show her the ring. "She also told me to watch over a set of books. So maybe that's what I'm hiding."

I skidded to a halt and said no more as I remembered what else she said. Gram told me that no one else could touch the books.

"I get it, Emme. It's your family duty to own this library. Why do you think my sister runs the coffee shop? My mom practically made her do it."

"I can understand how she must feel," I said sadly. I did understand, but this was way different. This duty of mine was more than running the library, but I couldn't find the words to explain this to Tarryn.

"Let's go to sleep. We have an early day tomorrow. I will tell you all you want to know, but it can't be tonight. Okay?"

"Okay." She nodded and I put the book back on the shelf.

She didn't ask more questions or intrude. She simply gave up. I just had to hope that she wouldn't bring it up again. I wouldn't leave Tarryn in the dark forever. She needed to know, and no matter how scared I was, I would tell her the truth. Eventually.

****

The library's grand opening was a success. All the children who came for story time were eager if not desperate for more stories. Tarryn ran the counter as I helped Mr. Gentry find a good stack of western novels that he could read. Most people told me how badly they missed my Gram and all of the books. Most of them were trapped in their homes for weeks on end due to the ice and snow. They needed their stories to help them escape from the harsh Maine winter. The children needed the story time and the indoor playground that Tarryn and I had put together. I used some of the extra funds, that somehow my Gram had set aside, to order plastic slides and foam mats. We set them up inside the largest room in the library. It was previously used for studying, but I decided that the kids needed it more. Those who wished to study could do so in the smaller room.

Watching the kids play put a smile on my face. If Gram could be here now and see this, I think that she would have been proud.

I looked at the many gifts the library patrons brought in to me as they visited and felt that they really missed Gram. I was confident that Tarryn and I were doing a pretty good job helping them enjoy the library once more. The money was not an issue and funds were coming in steadily from all over the place. It was like Gram either had a money tree at one time, or she was helping me as a ghost. I was getting checks from a library in Rhode Island on a weekly basis and it was all in Gram's name. I didn't ask questions; I just cashed the checks and put it into the library. Who was I to tell someone to stop paying Gram? I surely wasn't stupid. We needed the money, and it came.

We closed the doors at five 'o clock on the dot. I locked it and flipped the sign, and Tarryn drew the curtains.

"Well, I am going to just say that was pretty successful," Tarryn exclaimed after she was finished stocking the last book.

"I agree."

I shut down the last computer and flopped down in Gram's chair. Exhaustion was not the word for how tired I was.

"I'm going to run upstairs and take a shower. Then I'm going to bed. I never knew a day at work would be so exhausting," Tarryn told me after she shut off the reading lamps. "Coming?"

I shook my head. "I'm going to clean up the play room and read for a little while."

She smiled and nodded slightly.

Our awkward exchange from last night was never brought up again. She seemed to have forgotten all about it, and I wasn't bringing it up.

"Good night," I called as she left.

I leaned back in the chair and stared outside the window. The snow was starting to fall slowly, and I wondered when spring would arrive again. Would we be stuck in an eternal winter?

I tried to ignore the nagging feeling of the books below my feet. They were almost calling to me, begging for me to travel within them.

My skin longed to feel the sunshine of Jack's English home. I couldn't resist the temptation, so I clumsily dug them out of the floorboard. Instead of sitting in my nook, I entered the secret room.

I pulled the book open so fast I didn't have time to see if the title had changed since the last time I traveled. I began the chapter and felt the familiar feeling.

When I found myself staring at, not Jack, but a beautiful woman with the same eyes as me, I knew I had grabbed the wrong book.

Thirteen

Staring at me was Grace Bailey, my great-grandmother. She looked elegant and ethereal in a white lace gown that looked to meet the era exactly. Her curly hair was pinned up in a bun and she wore very little make-up. She looked so much like Gram it shook me to my soul.

Her smile was just like Gram's, and I smiled back. I mentally took a snapshot at that moment, hoping to capture a woman I had never met. This was so strange it was beyond any and all weirdness that traveling through the books had ever brought me before.

Meeting Nancy in the kitchen didn't compare to this. This was bizarro-land.

"Hello, child. I'm Grace. It's nice to meet you," she said with a smile. I noticed her lipstick had attached itself to her teeth just like my Gram's used to do. "You're a Bailey. There's no doubt about that. You have that Bailey look to you."

Her New England accent was as strong as Gram's, and it made me smile to hear it.

I tried to speak, but found that my damn voice wouldn't work.

"I know, child. It's a bit shocking to stare at your relative that should be...dead by the looks of your clothes. You're no doubt from the future. No way would any woman before me wear something so ugly."

I found my voice as I began to laugh. I was wearing a cream lace dress and my black tights and boots. I was not dressed ugly, but I guess if you came from the 1930s, you'd think this was hideous. Compared to her, I was the ugly duckling in the family.

I ran a hand over my dress then to my hair, hoping it was tame in my bun.

"You are beautiful, so don't fret. What's your name?"

"Emme," I choked. "Emmeline Bailey. I'm the granddaughter of your daughter, Mavis Bailey-Long."

Grace's eyes widened at my words.

"I have a daughter! What year is she born?"

"She's born in 1939, and she is a wonderful woman."

I didn't go into too much detail, but I explained how she met my grandfather and how they had my father. I told her how in love my grandfather was with the sea and how much he loved Gram that he decided to drop his own last name and take on hers.

"Well, Emme, the Bailey name is very important. I see that your father had it as well?"

I nodded. My father was a Bailey, even though his father's name was Long. Baileys *must* have been important because there was no talk of that ever happening anymore. When a man and woman married, traditionally, the woman takes his name. But for my grandfather, it wasn't that way. He loved Gram, and that was all that mattered.

I was proud to have the name. I always was. And I suppose my dad was too. He must have liked it better than Long as he went by Thomas Bailey, instead. I never questioned why he took Gram's last name; it was just something that never came up.

"If your grandfather was a Long, the family I'm thinking of, they came from a family of...well, misfits would be the right word for it. Maybe your father and grandfather were all right with giving up the name to spare them some embarrassment."

I shrugged.

I didn't know much of my grandfather's family, except that we never saw them. Dad never mentioned them before.

"Misfits, huh?"

She nodded. "The kind that do bad things and go to jail for it, for a long time."

I was catching on, now. They were bad people. Now I understood why my dad would not want to be associated with them. Dad had a good job—one where his name would be important. He worked at the law firm in the next town. If he was from a bad family, I could see why a name was important to earn people's trust.

I could hear sounds of talking and music coming from inside the house, and I realized that they were having a party. I also realized that we were standing outside Jack's home. It looked different to me at first because it was nighttime. The stars were beautiful as they shone down on the big house.

"They're hosting a little party in our honor," Grace explained. "You and me, we're going to go for a walk."

She took my arm in hers and we walked away from the noise and people.

"You're quite lucky you arrived when you did, otherwise you'd shock a whole lot of people. They all think we're visiting from America, which I suppose we are, but they're clueless we traveled through time, not by boat."

She laughed at her little joke and I smiled.

"I grabbed the wrong book. That's why I'm here. I have so many questions," I explained.

"I'm sure you do, and I will answer them all. But first, sit."

She ushered me to take a seat at a little white set of chairs that sat in a garden.

"You're probably confused. I know I was my first couple of times."

"That's an understatement. Most first times are awful, but at least we get a little warning. This one wasn't explained to me at all."

She frowned.

"You mean my daughter doesn't explain any of this to you? Not one bit?"

I shook my head, not wanting to tell her that her daughter died at the age of seventy-seven.

"She must not have the gift then. That makes me a bit melancholy, Emme. I'm sorry you're thrown into this life. But let me tell you, it's an important task and a huge responsibility that you've been granted."

Great! I need more responsibility on top of owning the library and promising to set aside my career. Let alone the college courses I've been taking at night via computer.

"The Bailey women have always had gifts of old magic. Not the kind you think of, Emme, but the kind that protect history. We are part of a secret society of travelers that maintain and protect the histories, which make the world what it is today. History can go back millions of years, and it is our duty to travel through the stories of old and capture every single moment.

"You see, Emme, we travel through books and capture moments that have yet to be told. We are not storytellers, but story-preservers. Many stories have been told of important times in history, and it is our job to travel back into time and live. We meet the people, and in those moments, it's all recorded."

I let her words roll around in my mind, just picturing the important moments in history. There were so many moments that happened it was overwhelming to believe that they were part of some of that. The fact that these women were able to see some of it was simply amazing.

"Which moments do you record, and why us?"

"Well," she paused, thinking, "the stories of influential men and women of history are most important. But we don't get to choose who or when. The books are handed down from family to family and we enter them at different times. You see, I'm here in this time and I'm capturing the history of a Mr. Jackson Ridgewell Sr. He is a very important man in our nation's history."

Jackson Ridgewell Sr. was Jack's father. I wasn't sure why he was important. I had never learned about him in our history text books.

I started bouncing my feet up and down, nervously, and biting my fingernails at the facts that swirled around me. I was scared and excited to be a part of something this huge. I had magic and was part of an elite group of story-preservers. This was way more than I thought it would be.

I had to confess to Grace. I had to tell her about meeting Jack.

"Are you all right, dear?"

"Yeah," I said as I forced myself to calm down. "It's a lot to take in. I have entered a time myself. Entering yours was, like I said, an accident. My time that I entered was 1892. I met Mr. Ridgewell's son, Jack."

"Oh, what a delightful boy he is. Tell me, does he grow up handsome?"

I wanted to tell her he was the hottest guy I've probably ever met, but realized that wasn't very proper. So I just said yes.

"You asked how we are able to travel, and I can't really explain the formula. That's up to the men who have written it, mostly scientists who have been assigned to our society to help us travel. It's all very boring stuff really," she said with a wave of her hand. "Harold Lockhart, he's been assigned to us Baileys for many years as his family was before him. He has the gift to travel back and forth to assist our ancestors."

I realized then that she was speaking of the group of women from the photograph: Jenny, Alice, and Laura. And I was right about Harold. He was, in fact, the one who helped them. While I liked being right, I wasn't going to be able to relish in it. I had questions, and I didn't know how much time I had left with her.

"Lockhart is a true talent. Like us, he is dedicated to preserving the histories and stories. He and I walked through the Salem Witch Trials together. Truly awful that was."

I shivered at the thought of being stuck there. I'd no doubt be captured as a witch and hanged on my first day all because of my choice of clothes. I didn't think they'd appreciate my many pairs of yoga pants.

"I know this is a bit much, Emme, but it's our duty to do this. Historians and researchers rely on us to learn. If we do not travel through the books and record what we learned, then think of what would be lost."

It's was a huge duty to do this and it wasn't lost on

me, but I wasn't sure I wanted it. I could barely handle meeting Jack, let alone meeting more people. The magic and everything was amazing, but I didn't know how far I wanted to be involved in this.

"I get that it's huge. I really do, but Gram left me her library. I was a college student, and I gave that up to take care of it. I can't do this forever, and I can't afford it either."

"Emme, you don't have to do this forever. And as long as you keep the library up and running, your money should keep coming. You'll never go broke." She laughed like the thought of a Bailey being poor was funny. Thinking about it now, I wasn't ever sure how Gram was able to raise me and the library too when I was a kid. I remember thinking that life as an adult meant endless money because Gram never ran out.

We never needed for food, clothes, or anything. Even when some of my friends' dads struggled to make ends meet, we never did.

If I needed new clothes, we got them. The time that I got my first car, it just appeared on my birthday. I never wondered how she did it, but now I knew the answers. "We take care of one another, Emme. All over the East Coast, the ones who are better off take care of the ones who aren't. And it seems like my daughter was the latter?"

I nodded and comprehended that she had referred to her own daughter in the past tense, like she knew she was no longer around. She understood that her daughter was dead, and I was all that was left.

"This isn't something you have to do for the rest of your life. You can stop and teach your own child when she's of age."

The thought of having a child made me almost violently

ill. I never thought I'd be the type of woman who was a mom. Losing my mother made me an awful and selfish person.

"Who is your protector?"

"My what, now?"

She giggled again. "You know the one who pulls you from the book after you travel. The person who is assigned to you to keep you safe."

The look on my face must have been a huge indication that I was totally clueless and had no protector because she stood fast, knocking over her chair. She looked terrified for me, and it scared the living hell out of me. I stood too, like that would somehow make this easier to explain.

"You don't have a protector?"

"Umm...no. I don't. What the hell is that?"

Her hands started shaking and she looked around us, terrifying me even more.

"Is a zombie going to jump out at us or something? What the hell are you doing?"

"Oh Emme, you could be stuck here. I'm so sorry this was never explained properly to you. You should have read the guide before you ever traveled."

Stuck here!

What freaking guide was she even talking about? I couldn't be stuck here. I had a life to get back to. I hated this time period.

No air conditioning. No ice-cubes. No cars. No cell phones. And to make matter's worse, Jack was only a boy still. He wasn't a man who I could end up falling in love with.

If he was, maybe I could swallow this news a little better. I'd stay with the book boyfriend and never leave. How awful would that be? But being as though he was probably twelve, I couldn't handle that.

"No! This can't happen. I have to get home. You have to help me," I begged her. My eyes filled with tears and I grabbed her hands. "What is the guide and where can I find it?"

She shrugged her shoulders and shook her head. How could I think that she'd know where it was in my time period? She could at least give me a hint of what it looked like, right?

Help me out here, lady!

"The set of books we all travel through have an instructional manual with them; it's a traveler's guide. When you travel, you must read that first. After you've traveled through your book, there are instructions on how to keep going or how to explain these steps to your children. Your protector, or guide, should be back in your year waiting for your safe return. She or he will have the guide book just in case things go wrong."

Great! Just great! Not only do I not have a guide, I don't have anyone back home watching over me to make sure I come back in one piece.

How on earth did I do this before and not stay stuck?

"Wait one minute!" I exclaimed. "I have traveled before. How could I have done that without a protector?"

Grace shook her head at me again with a bewildered look on her face. I wanted to slap her for getting my family into this mess. How dare she be this stupid book-magic wielder that only travels through time? Why couldn't she be a witch who conjures shit up? My family heritage was seriously lame, and I wanted to strangle my own great-grandmother.

"I traveled twice before this and each time I came out of it fine. That can't be coincidence, Grace. Throw me a bone here, lady. You have to know something," I pleaded.

"You had someone back there, in your time, watching over you, and you just didn't know it," said a voice behind me.

I swung around to see a handsome man with a black hair and the lamest mustache I'd ever seen. Somehow, though, it fit his face and made him look dashing.

Harold Lockhart.

"What do you mean?"

"I mean what I say," he said.

Smart ass.

I sat back down and racked my brain. The first time I traveled, I woke up to Rose shaking me. But she wasn't there the second time. Actually, no one was.

No! That's a lie. Someone was there, she was just upstairs.

"Can your protector change?"

"Sure. They just have to care for you," Harold replied. "They don't have to literally pull you out. All it takes is the force of a thought or concern."

The thought or concern for *me*.

"Tarryn," I mumbled aloud. "The first time it was my best friend, Rose. But the second time it was my roommate, Tarryn. She was upstairs."

"Well," Lockhart started, "she may have come to check on you and you didn't know it. I think you know your answer. Is this Tarryn with you now?"

What was he stupid? Did he see her?

Oh...he meant with my body in my time. That answered one question; I'm not sucked into the book and I don't disappear. I must be sitting there with my eyes wide open like Tarryn explained the other day. She must think I'm losing my mind. But all my other questions were still unanswered or confusing me still.

I nodded to Lockhart, hoping that Tarryn was indeed with me.

"I hope she checks on you because we're leaving soon."

Well, shit.

"When?"

Lockhart shrugged and said, "I'm not sure the time exactly. I just know it's soon. Our protector is keeping track of time. We knew that we were only permitted two days here and those two days expire soon."

"Emmeline, it's important that you read the guide and follow the rules exactly," Grace said before I recognized the pull from my time tugging at my body.

"I'm leaving," I told them with a thankful smile.

Grace looped her arm in Lockhart's, and they waved at me as I was sucked back into my own time.

Fourteen

Being pulled back to my time was the best thing to happen that night. I had thought that I would be stuck there forever. Thankfully, Tarryn was indeed there watching over me. The bad part was that I had to explain to her who and what I was, when I wasn't one hundred percent sure of all of it. I had so much more to learn, and she would be learning with me, if she didn't run away screaming first.

She stared at me like she thought that I was crazy, but after I blinked a few times and smiled at her, she seemed to relax.

"You did it again," she said.

Here goes nothing.

"Yes, I did. And I have something to tell you. You were right about me hiding something," I revealed. I told her everything I had learned and how I first traveled through the book before Gram died. I told her how I met Jack and how dashing he was, leaving out the fact that I couldn't stop thinking about him. I didn't hide how beautiful Jack's home was or how awful Nancy was, which made her laugh enormously. "She made me take my clothes off and wear a corset!" Tarryn continued to laugh at me, which gave me hope that she wouldn't dash at that moment.

I showed her Gram's hidden room and the photographs of The Librarians. She didn't say much, just nodded here and there. When I showed her the books and told her I had to find the guide, she bit her bottom lip like she was dying to tell me something important.

"What is it, Tarryn?" I asked after I had just spilled my most important secret to her.

"I found a book I think was meant for you, and I think it's your guidebook. I didn't mean to take it, but you weren't being honest with me and I knew it was important."

She pulled out a small pocket size book and handed it to me. It was in fact the guidebook. It may have been small in size, but it was thick with information. There was handwriting in it that had been from the women who traveled before me. Grace also had her own sections.

I never missed this book or knew that I needed it until it was in my hands. Once I held it, it was like I was reunited with an old friend. It was the strangest feeling I had ever experienced. I didn't question it, I just went with it.

"Where did you find this?"

"It was in your Gram's personal library upstairs. I wasn't snooping, it just sorta found me. I'm glad it did. You can't travel without your ring," Tarryn told me. "I read this book from cover to cover. Twice."

She laughed nervously, but I was so happy that I hugged her. She let out a little squeal, but eventually hugged back.

So my family members were using science to travel through time, and I was one of them. I was a traveler now. The truth was a bitter pill to swallow, but I would get to know my ancestry and would do them honor. They were the only family I had left.

"I'm so glad you don't think I'm crazy."

"I'm happy you're not crazy, too," she admitted. "The book explains why you are able to travel, and it's amazing actually."

We sat on the floor of the room and she turned the pages of the book.

"It's all here. Your ancestors have travelled as far back as the history of Egypt and the building of the pyramids. They travel to record what really happened and to make sure that history is exactly fact and not fiction. It explains that some historians tend to tell stories that haven't happened. Your family made sure this didn't occur. A book can be rewritten if it needs to be."

I pondered this and wondered how many books they've traveled through to ensure the truth was recovered. Just how many books were based on fact and not on the author's way with words?

"There are Librarians all over the world; some do different things. Your family is the only one to preserve history. Some travel back into books to make sure things are carried out exactly as they should and others find missing artifacts. There are entries from all of these women in the photo and some that aren't in the photo."

She pointed to Jenny's face and said, "Jenny got stuck inside a book on purpose."

My mouth fell open in shock. Who would do that? I could imagine getting lost inside the pages, sure, but to stay there forever wasn't for me.

"Did it say why?"

She shook her head. "Only that her protector, Beverly, was devastated that she did it. She traveled without telling her and she couldn't get her back. She tried real hard to retrieve her, but failed."

Maybe she fell in love with someone. Maybe, like me, she longed to be with him.

"When you travel, your physical self stays here while your spiritual self leaves. As long as you have your ring on, you are tethered with *your* time. If you take it off at all inside another time period, you could get stuck there," she explained further. "When the ring is removed, your whole physical self leaves. It's amazing, really."

I remembered her telling me how I looked like I was sleeping with my eyes open when she found me the first time. Now I understood perfectly. I was inside the book spiritually and physically anchored here.

"Tell me more about Jack. What does he look like?"

"He's probably the hottest guy I've ever met," I admitted. I could go on and on about how debonair Jack was. I was afraid to tell Tarryn about how much he consumed my thoughts.

"So he's the guy you spoke about at the bar, right?"

I nodded.

She sighed. "Let's Google him!"

"Let's not. I'd rather not find out by some website what happens to him. It's my job to record his history, not Google's."

She nodded in understanding, but I could see the disappointment in her eyes.

"I'll travel and get a photograph of him, okay? I'll bring this," I said as I lifted my cell phone. "I'll snap a nice picture of him. He would probably think it was amazing."

"Oh my God!" she exclaimed loudly. "You're in love with him, aren't you?"

I scoffed, "No way. I don't even know him. And he's

dead, Tarryn."

"Say what you want, but you have the look of love in your eyes," she teased.

"Well, you're gonna have the look of a black eye if you keep that up," I warned, jokingly. "Really, I need to travel back and see him soon. I have to keep recording his history. It's important."

She nodded and got up and stretched.

"Just not tonight. I'm tired and I don't feel like being your protector anymore tonight."

The guide specifically stated that I needed to officially ask someone I trusted to take the job of my protector. I hadn't known her for very long, but Tarryn was a great person. She was the sort of person I would trust with my life. She'd already studied the manual without being asked, and she was good with crazy. Anyone who was okay with all of this information was my kind of girl.

"Tarryn, before we go to bed, I want to ask you something," I began. I took a deep, nervous breath, and continued. "Would you like to be my protector? I mean, I know you are already sorta involved, but I think that I trust you. And I need to trust someone, strongly, if I'm going to do this. I can't do it alone, you know?"

She smiled and nodded her head before crashing into me with a hug that was so very unlike her. Maybe Tarryn needed purpose in her life, and I had just given it to her.

Fifteen

I ran the streets of Bay Ridge wearing the warmest workout clothes I could find. I hadn't run since I got here, and I yearned to feel that burn in my lungs and the familiar ache in my muscles. Running relieved a lot of stress for me, and without it, I was a ball of nerves. I rounded my first corner and prayed that I wouldn't slip on any hidden ice. So far, so good. I always ran in California, but it was way different running here. The weather in Maine did not always make it easy. I missed my campus's running paths, but the view of the ocean from where I was at that moment was breathtaking. Nothing compared to overlooking the wild and dark Atlantic Ocean this early in the morning.

Things were feeling semi-normal lately, and it was time to start being normal Emme. The library was up and running, and our first week went by in a flash. I was continuing to receive funding from what I guessed were other Librarians in our sect helping out. I was thankful to them, but wasn't sure what I could give in return. What did I have to offer them? Absolutely nothing, that's what.

I hadn't seen Jack since I met with Grace and I was dying

to do so. I had to record his history, and that wasn't lost on me. My duty to fill the pages of the book literally called to me now that I knew my purpose, but I desperately wanted to see him for another reason.

I wanted to feel wanted by him. The last time I was with him, it was brief, but he made me feel attractive. I hadn't been with a guy since I was in California. I wanted to feel special, and he did that. Sure, ripping his clothes off would be fabulous, but he was different. He didn't look at me like a conquest; he looked at me like I deserved to be cherished.

As I ran through the small park, I felt my lungs burn with that lovely feeling. It reminded me that I was alive. I took the turn and headed back to the library where I would wake a sleepy Tarryn. We made plans and I wasn't going to miss it.

****

Tarryn and I made sure all of the blinds were closed before I opened the book. She nervously settled down in the nook with me, holding the guide. I eased her fears and told her it was going to be fine twice already, but she was still anxious.

"I know what I'm doing," I explained softly. "I feel more confident this time."

I did. It wasn't a lie. I couldn't explain it; it was just a feeling I had that everything would be okay.

She held up her timer and nodded. We agreed that it was important to clock the amount of time I was gone from this world and to report on anything strange that happened to my body. Tarryn could handle this part, and I trusted her vehemently.

"I'm too nervous to talk right now. Just go," she urged.

"Okay. See you in a little while," I said, and I fell into the pages.

Sixteen

I was standing in a field. Alone.

I twirled around, and all I could see was more field, stretching as far as the eye could see.

Something was wrong.

There was no Jack and no grand house. The urge to cry or run was clawing at me from inside. I tried to calm myself down as I walked straight ahead of me, searching for signs of life. I heard a sound coming from ahead but wasn't sure what it was. It was a clicking noise that I couldn't distinguish.

I walked until I could hear it clearer, and I knew exactly what it was—horses.

The clip-clop of hooves was dead ahead of me. They sounded like they were actually coming closer to me, so I stood to the side and hoped they held a nice stranger. A stranger that wasn't going to notice a girl out of her time-period.

I looked down at the clothes Tarryn and I had picked out before I came. Tarryn read a chapter last night that explained the important of *dressing the part*. Guess I totally failed that part previously, but it wasn't too late.

The flowy dress we found at Goodwill fit me well, but with the summer sun bearing down on me, I was not feeling it. I was worried the sweat was ruining my whole proper lady look.

I looked up to see two brown horses coming through a small road that was completely hidden between a row of trees. Behind them they carried a large brick red coach. I hoped silently that it didn't hold anyone that would do me any harm as it neared.

I waved my hands at the driver and he waved back. He approached slowly, reigning in the scary horses, and greeted me with a smile.

"Greetings, my lady," he said politely with an English accent.

The doubt I had earlier about my whereabouts were erased; I was back in England.

"Uh ..." *Crap what was I supposed to do again?* Tarryn's words echoed through my frazzled brain. *Curtsy and smile bashfully.*

Even though I was awful at it, I did as she instructed and said, "Greetings, sir. I'm looking for an estate and seem to be turned around. I'm looking for the Ridgewell's."

I wasn't acing conversation in this era, that was for sure. I just prayed he would point out the way to Jack's house and save me more embarrassment. I silently thanked Tarryn for putting the hideous hat on me that she found on a mannequin in the Goodwill. I hated it when we bought it, but it was hiding my red cheeks at the present moment and that was a good thing.

"Ridgewell, well that's an hour that way, my lady. May I be of service and give you a ride in my coach?"

That voice. That was not the driver. I looked up and saw Jack hanging halfway out of the coach, holding his hand out to me. I ran to him before I had time to think about my actions and grabbed it. He kissed it gently with those full lips of his and welcomed me inside his ride. I rubbed my hands on the blue velvet seats.

"Very fancy," I exclaimed. I looked up at his eyes as they searched my face like he was memorizing each and every part of me.

"How long has it been?" I asked. I had arrived at different times in his life before, and I didn't expect anything different this time around.

"Only one week. I must admit it's been dreadful. I awaken and search for you everywhere, expecting you to be there. When I go to sleep, I'm full of sorrow that you've never arrived."

My heart stretched at his words and I wanted nothing more than to kiss his beautiful mouth.

I leaned over and gently placed my lips on his—feeling an electric pull inside me that I never had before. He ran his fingers ever so softly across my cheek as he leaned into me. I didn't know what I expected with a kiss from Jack, but it wasn't this. I didn't think he would kiss me back, being the proper English gentlemen. I also didn't think he would press into me with such fervor. Before things got too heated, he pulled back and my stupid hat fell from my head.

"I'm sorry, Emmeline. I shouldn't have," he said. I stopped him from saying anymore with a quick kiss.

His smile was so big it lit up the coach. "I want to treat you with respect. It was never my intention to be so forward."

I could eat him up, he was so adorable.

"I know that, Jack. But where I'm from, a kiss *is* respectful.

I have missed you. I don't understand my feelings for you yet, but I know that I think of you all the time."

He took my hand in his and kissed it. "I was just riding in this dreadful coach thinking about you and then, well, here you are."

I sat back into the plush seat and wondered where Jack was headed. Then it dawned on me—America. He was packed and ready to leave. I looked behind us and saw a large trunk strapped to the coach.

"You're going to America, aren't you?"

He nodded.

"I thought that I wouldn't get to see you before I left. I was terribly worried. I think I gave poor Nancy grief that she couldn't handle before I set off. In her words I spoke so much of you that she was going to lose her mind." He smiled again and I giggled like a silly school girl with a crush on the hot, new British guy. "How long will you visit this time?"

I shrugged my shoulders. "I don't know how long, Jack. I don't want to think about it though. I just want to spend time talking to you." I wanted to make up for lost time. "I figured out why I am able to visit you, though."

"Oh?"

I shifted in my dress and tried to get comfortable. It was impossible in this awful heat.

"It turns out I am part of a group of Librarians with a rare talent to travel through books," I began, leaving out the words *magic* and *science* for fear that he would frighten and push me from the coach. "We have a duty to meet with influential people and document our time with them. Actually, by being here with you, it's all being copied to text right now."

Placing his hand on his chin, he seemed to ponder this news. It was a lot to take in, especially for someone who wasn't used to this sort of thing. My era was a little bit more open to possibilities of this kind, but not his. The people of his time were a bit more sheltered.

"So, I'm to be influential?" he asked with a teasing smile.

"Well, I suppose you are. But I haven't really Googled you yet, so I don't know much about your future or why."

"Googled?"

"Uh ..." How was I supposed to explain that? "It's a place where you can find information on pretty much everyone and anything."

He nodded and said, "So it's like research. I understand. Forgive me, Emmeline, but why me? Why not my father?"

Why didn't he believe me? Jack's father, surely, was an important man, but I wasn't sent here for him. Jack had gone on and on about his dad and how he had to do what his father told him.

"Jack, if he was the person I was meant to meet, I would have. I researched my role in this crazy time-travel talent, and I'm here for you and you alone."

He shook his head and looked away from me and out at the trees beyond. His expression confused me. I hoped he wasn't unhappy with me.

"I'm sorry, Jack" was all I said.

"No, Emmeline," he said as he looked me in the eyes again. "Please don't be sorry. I just don't understand. Jackson Ridgewell Sr. is a man of good faith and honor, and I must follow in his footsteps. Perhaps I do become what you say. For now, tell me more about what you've learned. I do not know how much time I have with you."

I nodded, happy that he wasn't angry with me for what I said. Sometimes I had a real talent to put my foot in my mouth.

"So your name is really Jackson then?" It was rhetorical really, because I remembered hearing this before.

He nodded. "But I go by Jack."

"And I go by Emme, but you insist on calling me Emmeline. Why is that again?"

He was silent, thinking for a moment, and he said, "It's proper to call you Miss Bailey, but your name is stunning, like you."

I wanted to kiss him again, but I restrained myself. Trying to be a good girl was difficult. I surely could not fit in well in this time period. So, I told Jack all about the library opening and how Tarryn was helping me. I also told him about meeting my great-grandmother, and before I knew it I could smell the ocean. I looked up to see a port in front of us. Jack pointed out toward the sea at a large boat and said, "That will take me to America."

The boat was nothing like any I'd ever been on. Instead it looked like the damn Titanic, and I worried that it was going to go down with Jack on it. Thoughts of Jack clinging for life on the side of a sinking ship made me sick to my stomach. It couldn't be sturdy and handle such a trip, could it?

"That's the Lydia, and she's going to take me to Maine," he said as the coach stopped and the driver hopped down. I was thankful that the Lydia wasn't actually the Titanic. Maybe Jack would safely arrive in Maine after all.

The driver unstrapped the large trunk and began hauling it around to hand to a few men who would load it on the ship.

"I'm afraid that I only have one ticket, Emmeline." He held up a piece of paper as proof. "I'll make sure that my driver takes you back to the estate. You will be safe with him."

Oh. I couldn't travel with him.

"That's okay. I'll be fine," I lied.

Was I going to be fine? I would be stuck here watching the Lydia sail away with my dream guy and hoping that I got out of the book in time. I looked around at the shifty crowd standing by the docks and I suddenly didn't want to get out and walk around.

"Jack," I said nervously. "I can't exactly be seen like this."

I gestured to my crappy attire that didn't fit in with the style at all. It hadn't gotten past me that I might be the only woman on the docks that day.

"Like what...oh dear. You're correct." He placed the hideous hat on my head and it fell awkwardly over my face. "Well, that didn't help did it?"

"No. It didn't." I took the hat and threw it out the window. Jack laughed, and I realized I loved the sound of it.

"At least you're not wearing those ..., what do you call them? Oh! Yoga pants." The way he said it made me laugh hysterically.

"I will never get used to you, Emmeline. You are so surprising. I wish I could take you with me on my journey," he said, grabbing my hand in his.

I did too. But we both knew that wasn't going to happen. I wasn't sure if I'd see him after this.

Don't think like that.

I knew darn well that Jack's story didn't end here. He was important and his story was just beginning.

The ship made an awful sound, causing me to jump.

"Master Jackson, the ship is boarding. I will take the lady to her destination, but you must go," the driver insisted.

Jack stepped out of the carriage and said, "Take her back to the estate, Charlie."

Charlie nodded.

Jack leaned into the window and placed his two hands

gently on either side of my face, caressing it softly with his thumbs. His touch did all the right things, and at that moment it made me want to do all sorts of things—the sort of things to make Jack blush.

Remembering the photo I promised Tarryn, I pulled my cell out of a small pocket.

"I want to show you something amazing," I said as I held it up and snapped a quick picture of his smiling face. I turned the screen and showed him himself, smiling back.

"Wow, what is that? Is that...is that me?"

I nodded and explained, "It's a cell phone, but it captures pictures too. It does a lot of amazing things actually. But I wanted a photo of you."

"Will I see you again?" he asked. His eyes looked so sad and his mouth almost pouty. It made me want to stowaway in his luggage and travel with him. Well, to be honest I didn't do ocean travelling, due to my intense sea sickness, so book traveling was probably more my taste.

"I hope so." I couldn't make any promises. I didn't know if I would see him again. Traveling was so unpredictable. I wouldn't know at which point in his life that I would be seeing him next. Would he be married with children or still the young vibrant Jack? That was the awful thing about this whole talent.

While I was happy it had brought us together, I couldn't help but think about how it would rip us apart. I had to end this before anything really happened, to spare my heart and his. It was the best thing to do. Nothing good could come of a love affair with him. He was a man that I could never be with.

I had never felt this way for any man in my life, and the mere fact that I fallen for a guy that lived over a hundred years before me was so messed up, it was ridiculous. Of course I would fall for the unattainable man. I was so afraid of commitment that I couldn't be with a guy from my own time.

"Jack," I started. How could I tell him that we had to end this *thing* between us? It wasn't going to be easy, especially with the way he was looking at me at that moment. "I think that we should part ways—"

As the boats loud horn sounded again so noisily, it drowned out the rest of my words. He nodded and kissed me softly. I knew then that he hadn't heard what I said by the gleeful look in his eyes.

"Until next time, Emmeline Bailey!" he called over his shoulder as he walked away from me. It was then that I felt the tug from of my time pulling me back. So I let go.

Seventeen

"Two hours and forty-seven minutes," Tarryn said as I blinked my eyes to see her clearly.

"What?" I asked, confused.

"That's how long you've been gone." She waved the stopwatch in front of my face. "It's been so long, Emme. I thought you were dead, except for the fact that you were breathing. Oh God, Emme, it's awful sitting here watching you."

She grabbed me before I knew what was happening and hugged me, hard. I could feel her trembling as I hugged her back. She was terrified, the poor girl.

"I'm so sorry I scared you, Tarryn. But look at me, I'm fine," I said gently. She pulled back and nodded as a tear escaped her eyes. "I am all in one piece. But I'm famished."

She laughed and said, "Let's go get food into you then. And I want to hear about it all.

****

I had to drive to Larrison, the next town over, to deliver

my college essay in person and to sit for a test. Larrison Community College was *not* a prestigious school nor was it anything like my old school, but it was all I had here.

Bay Ridge didn't have a college so driving here, even if it was forty-five minutes away, was my only option. Gram's truck took the twists and turns with ease, but I couldn't go over fifty in this old beast. She was still running, just not as well as she used to. Winter gave way to spring as the wet icy roads melted and brown trees turned green. I loved this time of year when animals woke from their lazy slumber and flowers blossomed. I just wished I could escape the library more often to enjoy it.

I hadn't seen Jack for over a week and I was itching to travel soon. The library demands were keeping Tarryn and me from finding a free night to ourselves. Rose was over almost every night lately since her and the guy from work ended their relationship. Rose was the one to finally call it quits because she found out he liked the nurses just a little too much. He hadn't cheated, but according to Rose, he might as well had.

I didn't ask or pry for more; instead I played my best friend role and supported her. While she was with me, traveling was impossible. Unless I wanted to involve her in my secret, and I wasn't going to do that. She was my best friend, the one I told all my secrets too, but I couldn't tell her this one. Not only was it forbidden in the guide, but she wouldn't understand if she even believed me at all.

So for now, it was me and Tarryn, and I was okay with that.

My cell rang as I pulled into Larrison's parking lot. I put the truck into park and answered.

"Hello?"

"Oh, hi! Miss Bailey?"

"Yeah." I didn't look at caller ID when I probably should have.

"This is Jason at JR builders. I'm glad I got ahold of you, finally. We haven't had time to talk recently, and I wanted to know if you have been getting my messages."

Ugh, this guy again! I had been dodging his calls for months. I didn't want to sell Gram's property to him or to anyone.

"Listen, Jason, I told you before that I'm not selling, and I meant it. Please stop calling me."

I poised my finger over the end call button as he said, "Please reconsider, Miss Bailey. Our family has been in this area a long time. My great-great grandfather founded Bay Ridge in 1893."

My mouth dropped open as I pulled my finger back.

"What...what did you just say?"

There was a pause before he repeated himself.

"I said my family founded Bay Ridge. Over a hundred and twenty years ago. So we've been trying to preserve the land."

"By building freaking malls on it! You disgust me! I'm sure they would have been so angry to see what you tore down and built over it with. You know, I have an eye for beautiful things, Mr. whatever-your-name-is, and I can tell you that your shopping malls are *not* beautiful."

His laugh sounded through my phone so loudly that the speaker crackled. It wasn't funny at all, and the fact that this jerk-wad was laughing at me, made me as angry as a hornet.

He wasn't doing his family proud. They had come here, from God-knows-where, and they started a life. They started a home for many and this guy was making money off of tearing down those homes.

"You should be ashamed of yourself, Jason," I said clearly, with no shame. "You say you're trying to preserve Bay Ridge, but you want to take away a piece of history. My Gram's library has been around for several generations. Mr. Harold Lockhart was the first to own it, and he was magnificent. You should do your homework."

"Oh, should I? And what, Miss Bailey, should I research?"

"Try the term *asshole* first. Then after you learn a bit about *yourself*, learn about what real historical preserving is. Now goodbye!"

I ended the call with a fierce slap so hard the phone went flying. I didn't care. I was so flustered, and late for my class, that I fumbled out of the truck and left it behind.

****

My hands hadn't stopped shaking until I finished my exam. I should probably have skipped it all together after that phone call. His arrogance was a little too much for me to handle, so I texted Rose, asking her to meet me at the coffee shop for some much needed advice.

She got there before me, and I could see her inside talking to Tarryn. I put the truck into park and got out. The sun was shining, but it did little to brighten my mood.

"Hey! How did the test go?" Tarryn asked, handing me a cup of coffee.

I sighed. "I'm not so sure I passed. It was brutal."

With Rose here, I couldn't go into too much detail about the reasons why. I just really wanted to see my friends and see some semblance of a light at the end of the tunnel. With JR Builders on my back constantly, I found it hard to *want* to stay in Maine. I could preserve the stories anywhere. I didn't need to do it in Gram's library. As long as I had her ring, I could follow my dream and move to England like I always wanted.

"So, I have been hounded to sell the library," I blurted before taking a sip of my coffee. Tarryn's face fell but not Rose's.

No, her face looked almost happy. Rose always supported my passion to fly free of this place, but for her to look delighted at me selling the library shocked me.

"Are you happy about that, Rose?" I found myself asking her sarcastically.

She nodded and her mouth fell open slightly. "Don't get me wrong, I will miss the old place, but it's such a great location."

The old place?

I knew that I wanted an out, but I also wanted someone to fight to keep me here too. Was that wrong? I wasn't sure.

"A good location for what exactly?" Tarryn asked bluntly. I could see in Tarryn's face the same look I wanted to give my friend.

Rose fumbled for words before finally saying, "I didn't want to say anything to you after your Gram's death. It wasn't the right thing to tell you after that. But I want to open my own office here in town. I have my own dreams too, you know."

Rose did have her own desires, but I had no idea they included knocking down my library and building a strip mall and a doctor's office for her.

"I'm the best cardiovascular surgeon in this region, not to mention the youngest and the only one for miles. I want to open my own office to see patients outside of the hospital.

These heart patients have to drive two hours to see a doctor in an office."

It was true; she was the best. But it was also true that the library helped residents. Not on the same level of course, but we were the only entertainment for many.

"You don't even want to be here, Emme. Don't pretend like you wanted to come back to Bay Ridge. If your Gram wasn't dying, you'd still be in California with all those snobs you called friends!"

Whoa! That was it.

"Rose, I'm going to pretend like you didn't say the last part because I've had a really shitty day," I stated as I stood up to gather my purse. My hands shook slightly as adrenaline coursed through me. "I understand that you want things for this town, but I do too. I wanted to help this town after Gram died. I had a duty to fulfill and I'm doing it. I refuse to sell it to *anyone* so they can build a strip mall and ruin one of the last historic buildings in Bay Ridge."

Tarryn stood then as well and gathered her things.

"I may not have had plans to move back here, but I'm here now, and I'm not going anywhere," I said. "Oh, and as for those snobby friends of mine, I wrote them out of my life like that." I snapped my fingers and Rose's eyes blinked. "I can do that with just about anyone who calls themselves my friend while at the same time stabbing me in the back."

I left with Tarryn and didn't give Rose a second glance.

Eighteen

My day was awful, and I refused to let my night be the same. I took Jack's book upstairs with me and crawled into bed. With or without Tarryn, I was traveling to see him, and I didn't care about any consequences either. I flipped open to the last marked page and felt myself being whisked away from this world and all its drama.

His eyes were the first thing I saw, so vibrant even in the darkness that they made me literally swoon.

"Emmeline, you're here," he whispered before he hugged me to him. Before I could expect it, he kissed me fiercely like I was water and he was dying of thirst. I let him take me away from all my worries as I kissed him back. I didn't know where we were, and I didn't care. I ran my fingers through his curls and down his back. He let out a moan and that was all I could take; I pushed him and he fell back upon a large bed. The room we were in was only lit by the light of a fireplace, making him look so handsome. We were going fast, but I didn't think about it too much. I needed him, and I felt that he needed me just as bad as I straddled him. My hair fell across his face, tickling him. He ran his hands down my back and when they came up, he gripped onto me like he was clinging on for dear life. We were going way past a make-out session in his carriage at this point.

"Emmeline," he whispered again, sending shivers through my whole body. "I want to be with you so badly that I'm not sure I can keep going without you. These days spent wondering if you will arrive had me going mad. You nearly gave me a fright appearing out of nowhere like this. But I shan't complain one bit more."

If he was scared, he didn't show it. The reception he gave me was that of hunger, not fear.

I sighed, "I'm so sorry that I can't be with you more, and I wish that I could be. I never know when I'm going to be able to get back here to be with you, and each time I do, I leave even more devastated than the last."

I sat up and looked at him, drinking him in. He was wearing a white shirt, untucked from his pants. The fabric fell loosely around his muscular body.

"Emmeline, I must be frank with you about something," he said as I began running my hands along the soft fabric.

"You can tell me anything."

I loved the way he looked at me like I was the first girl he'd ever seen. It made me feel special, like the most beautiful thing in his life.

"I'm not quite sure how to put this," he mumbled as I kissed his neck.

"Am I going too fast? Do you not want to be with me like this?" I sat up fast.

It would be just like me to scare a guy away by going faster than he was ready for. I didn't want him to think I was some sort of hussy, but I couldn't help my feelings for him. I wanted him to see all of me, and I wasn't scared of spending the night with him. Whether he was or not, was the real question.

He sat up and I slid back onto the bed and off of him. He put his hands on my face, cupping my cheeks.

"Fast might be a good word to describe it, but," he leaned in closer and said, "don't ever think for a moment that I do not want you, Emmeline Bailey. In fact, I'll have you know, I have never wanted a woman as much as I want you. And there have been others who wanted me to court them, but I never felt for them as I do for you."

"Then what is it?" I asked as I hugged myself, feeling instantly shy.

"Premarital relations are frowned upon in *my* time."

Shit. Stupid me. I had totally forgotten the rules of dating in this era. Coming here I wanted to get away from my troubles and lose myself in his arms, and I pushed him away instead.

Suddenly, it dawned on me that Jack was probably a virgin. The way he was studying me didn't give me that vibe though. Surely not the way he kissed me or caressed me; that was the work of a man who knew what he was doing.

I couldn't ask him. I was embarrassed enough that I came here and attacked him like I had.

The way he was looking at me at that moment made me shiver once again, and I leaned forward, enclosing the space between us. Daring him, just to see how far he would go.

"I would never ask you to give up your beliefs, Jack. I can't deny how I feel about you. I've never felt this way about any guy, ever," I confessed. Saying the words to him was a relief. "I'm sorry for throwing myself at you when you're not ready. I would never want you to do something you weren't ready for."

He closed his eyes as I spoke and licked his lips. Jesus, Mary, and Joseph, he was making this hard for me. As much as I wanted to back away and give him some space to calm down, I couldn't bring myself to do it. He opened his eyes, and I could see a hunger there like I've never seen before. He brought his hand up and put it on my shoulder, drawing light circles all the way down to my hand. He took my hand in his and kissed it.

"I'm yours, Emmeline, if you'll have me. I want no other woman but you," he told me before he kissed me gently on the lips. "I want to make you happy in any way that I can."

I wanted to be happy. He made me feel elated and light in his arms, and I didn't want to change that.

As he trailed kisses down my cheek and neck, I let my hands wrap around his. He lifted me from the bed and we stood together, looking at each other like it was the first time. I pulled his shirt over his head and threw it aside. His gloriously built body made my heart pound. He was beautiful, especially in the glow of the firelight.

Off came my shirt and gently he tried to take off my bra, but I soon realized he had probably never seen anything like it before. I helped him, and it landed on the floor at my feet.

"What on earth was that?" he asked with a laugh.

"It's called a bra. Trust me it's not as sexy as a corset, but it feels better."

"Everything on you is smashing, Emmeline."

He ran his hands over my breasts as if memorizing the very detail of them. I wanted him so bad, but at the same time I didn't want to rush. I wanted to take my time with Jack. His light feathery kisses ran from my chest down to my tummy. As he came to the button of my jeans, he looked up at me puzzled. I shrugged.

"May I?"

Hell yes, you may.

I nodded and he ripped the top so hard the button flew off and across the room. A laugh escaped me but stopped when he pulled my jeans down, and he looked up at me. His serious face didn't betray him. He wanted me, there was no denying it.

How could I have thought differently? My heart knew the truth.

My lace panties were the only thing left on my body. I wanted to rip them off, but Jack had other plans. He stood and lifted me again, this time, lying me gently onto the bed. I could feel the heat from the fireplace warming my already hot skin.

With a swift movement, I was the only one dressed in the room. Jack lay atop me and started kissing me gently, teasingly. "Emmeline," he whispered, "it's urgent that I confess."

"Anything."

He looked away from me, almost ashamed.

"Hey," I said, lifting his chin. "We all have a first time."

He nodded, confirming my suspicions that he was a virgin.

"It's okay," I told him. "I'm falling for you, Jack."

"I've already fallen."

There were no questions about me and my first time. No pressure. No feelings of regret.

He leaned down and held me to him. He was this beautiful man and he was experiencing his first time with *me*. I wrapped my legs around him, hooking them behind his back.

"Being with you makes me feel things I've never felt

before," he whispered. "I never want you to leave me."

I arched my back as I could feel the rushing heat between us. I didn't want to leave him ever again. I could just slip off my ring and not ever go back. I'd be able to be with him, here, forever. We fell into each other as if time between us didn't matter.

I let him explore my body like I was a land he had never seen before, and I taught him things he probably never knew. We were one, and that was all that mattered for the time being.

After we were finished loving each other, Jack fell beside me, his breathing labored, and stared at me in awe. His smile was so large, I wanted to take a picture of it and keep it forever. He was truly happy.

"Are you pleased, Emmeline?" he asked.

"Yes, Jack. Are you kidding? Seeing you happy is all I need right now."

He nodded and closed his eyes. I sat up and took in the beauty of his body in the light of the fire. This man was mine.

But I couldn't have him, could I?

He was mine in my heart, but not really. He had lived his life, and I was only an intruder in his story. I was supposed to be preserving the pages written about him, but instead I was taking his virginity and maybe ruining his future.

"What's wrong, Emmeline?" he asked, sitting up.

Tears came to my eyes, and I tried to hide them. Stupid emotions and reality ruined everything.

"Are you upset?"

"No, Jack. I'm just really happy, and I...I don't want to leave you again," I confessed. "I'm just a visitor in your life, but I want to be more."

He sat up and cradled me in his arms.

"What is stopping you then? Stay with me and never leave. Become my wife, and we'll start a family together. I can and *will* make you happy, Emmeline."

There was no doubt he would make my life good, so what was stopping me from ripping off the ring and staying with him?

I couldn't answer that question. All I knew was I had a foreboding feeling, and I didn't belong in this time with him. I knew that my love for him was real, tangible.

But our love wasn't supposed to happen.

"Let me please you, Emmeline. I can take the doubts from your mind," he said as he kissed me. Tears streamed down my face as he pulled me closer to him. "Just give me a chance."

I nodded and fell into his embrace. I lost myself again in his arms. He pulled me into a bliss I had never known. He taught me things about myself that I didn't think possible.

As he fell asleep, I rested my head on his chest. I could feel his breathing slow as he began to drift further and further into dreamland. I looked at the ring on my finger and realized at any moment I could be ripped away from Jack and the beauty of what we had made here. It was then that I took it off and put it into my pocket.

Nineteen

I woke to the sounds of people talking. I sat up quickly and pulled the covers up around my bare breasts. *Where is my shirt?* I wondered as it started to click that I wasn't at home, but instead with Jack. Wherever that was.

We talked about a lot of things last night, except for where he was currently living. I looked around the now cold room and Jack wasn't anywhere. The room looked dramatically differently during the day than it did last night. What I had thought was the most romantic setting was instead a basic and almost empty looking space. There were only a few pieces of furniture: a bed, a dresser, and a chair. The strangest thing about the room was there was a sink and wash towels. I wasn't expecting to see that in the room, and I hoped there wasn't a toilet in here too.

I got out of the bed and put on my shirt and jeans—checking to make sure my ring was still secure in the pocket, and it was. I ran the water in the sink and washed my face quickly. There was no hope for my hair, so I ran my wet fingers through it to calm the crazy wild curls, thanks to bed-head. I checked myself over in the mirror and realized that there was no way I would ever fit in looking like that, so there was no use in fixing my hair at all. Nothing I did to my hair or clothes at this point would work; I wasn't from this time and that was that.

I looked out the window hoping for some sign of where Jack was, but all I found was a rocky cliff overlooking the ocean, children playing, and women hanging clothes on a clothesline. I did a double take at the ocean and instantly opened the window to get a better look. As soon as I did, the smell of salty air hit me. We were in Maine. No doubt about it. I knew that salty sea air and that ocean.

"See anything you like out there?"

I turned fast to see Jack balancing a tray full of food with one hand and closing the door with the other. I rushed to his aid just in time to save a dish of grapes. He thanked me and set the tray down on the bed.

"I thought I would run out and get us a proper breakfast. I imagine you're famished," he said.

Thinking about it, I was hungry. We stayed up pretty late, and I hadn't eaten before I came here.

I popped a grape into my mouth and nodded as the fruit burst in my mouth. I didn't realize how hungry I was until then.

"These grapes are so good," I said before I put more in. "You really need some."

I held one out to him, and he opened his mouth, letting me feed him. His full lips took the grape and he sucked it in. The way he chewed it made me sigh. I had never known a man who could make eating so damn sexy.

"Do you like what you saw?" he asked.

"Excuse me?"

"Outside. Did you like the view?"

I laughed. Of course he didn't mean the view of him chewing.

"I always said I had an eye for beautiful things, and that view is more than beautiful. We're in Maine, aren't we?"

His face grew into a huge grin as he tapped me on the nose with his finger tip.

"How are you so intelligent, Emmeline Bailey?"

I shrugged. "I've lived here, there, my whole life. The Maine coast is the most beautiful. I mean not even California can compare," I told him as I shoveled a piece of bread into my mouth.

"California? What is that?"

I laughed and a piece of bread came flying out of my mouth. Always the graceful lady.

"California," I restated, saying slowly this time. "I guess you wouldn't know about it yet. But you will the longer you're here in the United States. You'll hear all about the Gold Rush that occurred."

He nodded like it sounded familiar.

"Yes, now it's ringing a bell. Someone was saying that their cousin went west in search of gold," he said.

He took his napkin and plated it gracefully over his lap before buttering his bread. "And you've been there?"

I put my bread down and copied his manners, putting my napkin over my lap. "I lived there. It's where I went to college, before ..."

"Ah, yes, before your grandmother passed away. Emmeline, you mustn't feel like you have to do as I do."

I looked up from my bread and said, "Huh?"

He pointed at me. "You're mimicking me. You do not need to do as I do; be yourself. That's what I love so much about you, how you're nothing like me. I was raised in a home where we had servants who followed us 'round the clock. My valet dressed me and opened doors for me. We sit at a table and are served food." He paused and sighed heavily. "I cannot even sneak into a kitchen to steal a tray of food without someone doing it for me."

Suddenly I felt sad for him. I was raised with a freedom Jack would never know. It was almost comparable to being a movie star. He lived a lush life that I looked at from afar and wished I had. But at the end of the day, I was happy in my little home because it was comfortable and it was mine.

"Where are we anyway? Is this your new home?"

He shook his head and waved his hand. "My father would keel over if he knew I was staying here. He thinks I'm on my way to his new estate in two days. I took advantage of the boat's early arrival and booked myself a small holiday here."

I nodded in understanding. He needed a breather before he was forced to be around his pushy father. I wished that I could bring him back through the book with me for those two days. Instead we had to make the best of the time we had together.

"I can stay with you if you want." I suddenly realized that taking off my ring might not have been a good idea. What if he wanted to be alone and not spend time dragging his futuristic girlfriend around?

"You can stay, here? How does that work exactly?"

I pulled the ring from my pocket and I placed it into his open palm.

"This ring tethers me to my time. Without it, I'm here and I cannot travel back until I place it back on my finger. Why don't you hold onto it for me?"

He looked at it and admired the gemstone.

"I may not ever give it back to you, Emmeline, for fear

of losing you again to the pages of a book." He put it on his pinkie and winked at me. "Will you be missed at home?"

I shook my head. "No."

Now that the ring left my hand, I was no longer there in body. My full self, spirit and physical, was here and all that would be left behind was the book. Hopefully Tarryn knew that I wasn't missing but instead with Jack. I wished I could get a note to her not to worry about me. I wondered whether time moved the same there as it did here, and if I would be gone for the same amount of days.

"Maybe missing for two days is a bad idea."

"Is it?" Jack asked looking up at me.

"Did I say that aloud?"

"You did, yes. If it's too long, you can go back tonight. I refuse to let you leave me now. I do have the ring, remember?" He held up his sparkly pinkie and wiggled it at me. "Let's make the best of the day. I would like to see the ocean today. Do you fancy a swim?"

I would fancy being with him again in this bed, but heck, I'd be down for getting into a bikini and going for a dip. Anything to get my body next to his.

"I'll need to change first. I can't go swimming in this, unless we go naked," I said with a wink.

He swallowed hard and stood fast, causing his food to fall on the floor.

"I'll get you someone...someone to give you attire. Even though, being bare with you would be a jolly good time."

I loved his accent so much. I'd show him a jolly time indeed.

As I stood in the hideous apparel the women of nineteenth century called swimwear, I realized Jack and I would not be seeing much of each other's bodies anytime soon. The swimsuit was a godawful piece of clothing that I compared to a tent. It didn't hug any of my curves or flatter any part of my body at all. It was navy blue and pinstriped. It wasn't even a pretty color. I wondered who designed this as I played with the bulky material.

"Ah, it fits you nicely, dearie," said the lady who put me into it.

I shook my head and replied, "I think it's too big."

She only cackled at me, like I told a hilarious joke.

"It's just your size, and if you ask me, I think it might show just a bit too much already. Anything smaller would be too risqué for a nice girl like you."

She continued to laugh at me as she left me alone in the room. I flipped her off, without her noticing, and turned to look at the rest of the clothes she left for me.

The dresses were gorgeous, but this thing, this was worthy of a match when I got back. For now I had no choice but to wear it.

Twenty

The beach was empty, except for a handsome guy standing in shorts and a striped shirt.

He waved at me and I waved back. I sure hoped he didn't think I looked as awful as I felt. When I made it over to him, he whistled.

"Do not tease me, Jack," I warned. I could feel my cheeks reddening.

"Emmeline, I promise you that I wasn't. You look absolutely smashing in that bathing suit."

I looked up and smiled. "Really?"

"Truly. You're gams are astonishing."

Gams? Oh, legs.

"Thank you. You look quite sexy yourself in this," I said as I ran my hands over his chest. He made his striped suit, which reminded me slightly of a prison jumpsuit, look dashing.

"Are you up for a swim?"

I was up for anything. I took his hand and he guided me toward the water. Looking out beyond at the endless sea, I couldn't help but feel foolish for worrying about how I looked. Jack saw me as a beautiful thing, and I had to say, he could wear anything and I'd still feel the same for him. I realized how my era was so behind in what was truly beautiful.

A swimsuit didn't make a girl pretty in his time. He was attracted to the real me, even though my body was completely covered in this tent, aka suit.

The cold water hit our feet, causing us to scream at the same time. I splashed him with a handful of it, and he glared at me teasingly.

"Oh, you're in for it now, Emme. I'm going to dunk you." He chased me around until he did dunk me.

We finally got tired of playing with the icy water and landed on the beach shivering.

Jack pulled a blanket over me and rubbed my arms gently.

"I'm not accustomed to spending time with a woman like you in public."

"What do you mean?" I asked through chattering teeth, trying to ignore the "like you" part.

"What we did last night, and just now, is considered poor manners and low quality. It would make me an improper man. I assure you, Emme, I am a gentleman," he said quietly. "I feel as if I'm dishonoring my name by being so forward with you."

He had been calling me Emme for the last hour or so, but I thought nothing of it until then. He had called me Emmeline up until we had sex, and I couldn't help but think that being *just Emme* now meant he didn't respect me.

Instead of dwelling on it, I tried to find the words to make him feel like the time we spent wasn't making him a horrible person, but I didn't know how to explain it in terms that he would understand. Instead, I just said, "Jack, compared to men in my time, you're of the highest quality. And you're the only man I have had feelings for."

He blinked.

"You cannot be serious, Emme. The only man?"

I shrugged. What could I say that would make him believe me?

"I don't exactly get close to guys. I stay away from relationships like this. I would have never gone to the beach after spending the night with a guy." I realized how much of a hussy I was making myself out to be. Jack must have registered this thought at the same time as I did. It was written all over his face. "I care about you very much, Jack. You're special to me. You mean more to me than any guy I've ever met."

He nodded and soon after looked away from me and focused his attention on the sea. I was losing his respect. I hated that I was being judged for my past indiscretions. If he was a lady's man, I wouldn't be able to evaluate his life without getting flack for it. Instead I'd hear, "Boys will be boys."

The fact was: I was in love with him now, and I was embarrassed about my past. But how did I tell him that in a way he would truly understand it?

"Please try to understand that it is socially acceptable in my time for a woman to want to have sex with a man and not get married right after. Women have certain needs too, not just men." This was going terrific so far, since he didn't even make eye contact with me. I took a deep breath and tried to bury the sarcasm. "Since my dad died, I didn't have a father figure in my life. Gram did her best to teach me about being a woman, but I didn't have a man to fulfill the role of protector. So, when it came to guys, I stayed far away. I pushed myself further and further away from any potential relationships. And I just dated casually. Is this like, a big deal to you?"

For a few seconds, that felt like minutes, he didn't say a word. I looked out at the raging ocean before us, wishing that I could slip my ring on and disappear. This was the most awkward situation I'd ever been in. I felt a tear escape and drop on my hand. I didn't usually cry over boys, but Jack was making me feel awful.

"I can't pretend I'm something I'm not," I choked out.

He finally looked at me, and I saw a storm in his blue eyes. "I am not asking that of you, Emmeline. I won't make you be someone you're truly not. It's just simply unheard of for such a lady, in high standings, to be...familiar with men in that way."

That hurt. A lot.

"So basically I'm the equivalent of a slut in your eyes?"

All I heard was a deep intake of breath from him and that was it. He didn't deny it. I had only shocked him more.

I got up from the sand and hauled ass away from him, and I didn't look back.

Once back at the hotel, my face was a mess. I could see all the women staring at me as I walked up. I tried to wipe away the tears, but I knew once I cried, my face would turn beat red and it was hard to hide. I finally made it to the room, ripping off the stupid bathing suit and throwing it across the room. It landed with a slap on the wall and slid all the way down to the floor.

I found my clothes and quickly got dressed. I needed to get back home and deal with my own life. This was the exact reason why I didn't let men into my life; I would get hurt.

I had a complicated duty now as a preserver, and that meant getting cozy with my subject was the worst idea I had ever had. Just because Jack was handsome didn't mean I should have jumped his bones. I should have just done my job and left it at that. But nooo, I had to fall in love with him. His actions on the beach had me questioning my real feelings for him. Was it really love or infatuation? What was the difference anyway? I couldn't answer that since I had never felt anything for a man before.

If he had real feelings for me, he wouldn't have ever talked to me in that way. That I do know.

I searched the room for my Gram's ring and realized Jack had it still.

"Dammit!" I yelled as loud as I could. The truth was, I was upset from my fight with Rose and I came here to see him, hoping it would make me feel better. That plan didn't work because now I felt worse. I tried to run away from my problems, and it did no good.

Jack had my ticket out of here, and there was no way I would be asking for it back. I lay on the bed and cried. I cried for the girl inside me that made stupid choices. I also cried for the college life I left behind in California. Sometimes I wished that I had just never come home, as awful as that sounded.

I cried until I couldn't stop my eyes from shutting. And then I fell asleep.

****

"Emme? Wake up, darling," Jack's voice pulled me from dreamland. After I had torn apart the room looking for the ring, I laid on the bed. I must have fallen asleep shortly after.

I sat up and rubbed my eyes; they were raw and painful from crying.

"What are you doing here?" I asked harshly.

He looked down at the floor and then back up at me. Guilt crossed his face.

"Were you looking for this?" He held up his pinkie finger and I saw Gram's ring.

Clothes were strewn about the room in a mad disarray. I didn't bother fixing anything that I ruined since I was so pissed. I wanted the ring and I wanted to go home. I never dreamed he wore it into the ocean on his finger. I rolled my eyes.

"Yes. I wanted to go home. I still do," I said simply.

He looked hurt, but I wasn't going to worry about sparing his feelings one bit. He didn't care about sparing mine.

"Listen, I will let you go, if that's really what you want."

"It is."

"Emmeline, first let me explain my actions on the beach. Please, I beg of you."

I crossed my arms defiantly and nodded. This had better be good.

"Thank you. First and foremost, I have been with a woman before you. We weren't as intimate as you and I were last night, but we were close. I stopped it before it went too far. I wanted to be with my wife for the first time, not someone I was courting."

I sighed and said, "Well, I'm sorry I was the one who ruined your perfect first time and your image."

He shook his head and cringed a little.

"Well, I'm not sorry it was you. Actually, I'm quite happy that it was. On the beach, I was just trying to explain the feelings of guilt I had. You don't have to understand why I feel that way, I just do."

I bit my tongue, trying to not say something sarcastic.

I had an issue with that. I pulled my legs up and closed my eyes. I had to try to understand Jack's point of view. If I was from his time, I would understand. I knew I would.

I opened my eyes and sat up. He looked so upset, and I could tell he was hurting just from the look on his face. Jack came from a noble family that honored women and made it their pride to be respectable men.

"Jack, you should have told me to wait. We could have, you know?"

He nodded and met my eyes. "Have you seen yourself? You're gorgeous. When you came here last night, I was in a bad way. I needed to hold you, and I sensed you needed that as well."

"But we didn't have to go so far, especially if you didn't want to. I can wait, you know. I'm not some sex fiend."

He made a face at me. "Sex fiend?"

I sighed. "Yeah, like I have to have it. I could have just kissed a little and let you hold me."

He scooted closer to me on the bed. I could sense that he was trying to go slow with me, not sure whether I was ready for him to touch me. So, I reached out and grabbed his hand.

"I had a bad day yesterday, too. I think I wanted to be held just as much as you did. But when I'm with you, it's not that easy," I explained. "It's like there is an electricity between us. It only intensifies when we kiss, and I couldn't stop myself. When you told me how you felt about me, well, it only made me want it more. I'm sorry for ruining your honorable past." I meant it.

I never meant to come here and screw up Jack's future. I couldn't help my feelings for him, but I could have not acted on them. I could have just come here and talked to him.

"Emme, I wanted you just as badly. And let us be clear,

you didn't act alone. I'm sorry for making you feel like a horrible woman. You are not what you said on the beach. Please never disrespect yourself again, darling."

I smiled. "I'll try." I could get really used to being called darling. The way it rolled off of his tongue made my heart melt. Jack may have thought that he had ruined his image by sleeping with me, but he was wrong.

"What do we do now?" he asked.

I thought about it for a moment. We still had all the rest of today to spend together and tomorrow. I could stay until then, but then I would still be hiding from the things I needed to go back to. I still had a life back there, even if I felt like Jack was pulling me into his. I couldn't escape from the truth.

"I have to go back home, Jack."

Twenty-One

Jack's face fell in disappointment. It was apparent that he didn't want me to go, but I had to. He handed me my ring and I held it in my palm. I wasn't sure if I would go back immediately after putting it on, or if it would take hours. I didn't risk it. I put it on the side table and faced Jack.

"I can go in a little while. Until then, let's talk about what's going on inside that head of yours," I suggested.

He took my hand and pulled me up off of the bed. "Let's go for a walk and I'll tell you all about it."

I nodded. My stomach growled loudly, realizing that I was starving. I hadn't eaten since breakfast.

"First, food," I demanded.

"Food, yes. But first, my dear, you must change your attire," he said pointing at my clothes.

"Turn around, then," I told him. He stood and turned toward the wall while I searched for the dress that the lady from earlier had laid out for me. It fit me well enough, a little loose in the mid-section, but rather pretty. I left on my own bra and underwear, opting for comfort instead of style.

I tried to fasten up the back as far as I could and realized I needed help from Jack.

"Jack, I'm going to need you for a moment," I said still struggling.

He turned around and smiled, taking me in. He walked around me and took the hook in his hands, tugging it up. Once it was fastened, he rested his hands on my shoulders and leaned closer to me, sniffing my hair.

"I can't help myself when I'm in your presence, Emme. I want nothing more than to help you *undress*."

I sighed and fell into him. I wanted the same thing, but I didn't want to put him into anymore turmoil. He was already battling with feelings I couldn't understand. So I turned and put as much needed distance between us.

"Jack, I'm here to learn about you. So let me do that, please. We need to eat."

He nodded and the pained expression left his face.

"Right. Yes."

If we got through this night without ripping each other's clothes off, it would be a miracle.

****

I could smell the food coming from the inn a mile away. The whole town was quiet up until we reached the town square. Men and women walked arm in arm talking and laughing as music wafted from the inn. I held onto Jack as a breeze blew across, taking my skirt up with it. I held it down and wished I was wearing pants and Uggs instead. Other women were dressed like me, except they didn't seem to mind the cold. I couldn't handle this cold and the billowing skirt around me. I needed warmth, so I leaned into Jack for it.

"Cold, love?" he asked as he ran his hand down my arm. "We're almost there. Just across the square." He pointed to a small building, and I nodded. I hoped it had some sort of heat inside.

"What is this town?" I asked, realizing that I never figured it out.

"Larrison," he answered.

My mouth fell open in shock and realization. My college would be in Larrison, sometime in the future. I looked around for some sort of familiar sign of the town I knew, but couldn't see anything. It was very possible that Larrison had changed dramatically over the years.

"Do you know it?" Jack asked.

"I do. I go to school here now."

He cocked his head trying to understand my meaning.

"I haven't told you," I began. "I started going back to school since I got settled with Gram's library. I am so excited to be able to finally get my degree and start the rest of my life."

Just thinking about finishing my schooling, made me smile. I was giddy with excitement that my life was going back to normal.

Jack's face seemed delighted too. He pulled me across the cobblestone street and into a small alcove, away from everyone else.

He drew me into him and gave me a hug. "I'm so elated for you, Emme. I know you'll make a great teacher. I hope you get all your dreams."

I closed my eyes and leaned into him. "Me too."

I was realizing that some of my dreams were right here in his arms. It was a problem I wasn't able to fix. I couldn't choose between Jack and my current life, and I didn't want to. I wished that I could merge the two.

"Jack," I whispered, "I don't want to be without you, but I have to leave. Does that make sense at all?"

He looked up at me, his eyes were shining bright in the darkness. "Emmeline, nothing makes sense since you've landed in my life. I still cannot fathom that a girl from the future holds a place in my heart."

I couldn't believe it either, but it was happening. We were making our own history; it was just a separate story. The story of Jack and Emme wasn't going to have a happy ending. We wouldn't make history books, and no one would know about us. "We were doomed from the start, weren't we? I mean, can it end happily?" I wished that he had the answers I didn't. His blank stare told me *no*.

"I do not know what to say, Emmeline. Only that I wish you could stay with me."

A lump formed into my throat as I fought the tears off. I wished that I could split myself into two.

"I can't leave my friend alone to run Gram's library. I just can't. I have a duty to run it and—"

He put his fingers on my lips, stopping me. "Shh, darling. No need to explain. I understand."

A tear slid down my cheek and Jack wiped it away.

"This will not be goodbye, Emmeline Bailey. Not today. Not tomorrow. Not until it's truly time, understand?" I nodded and he smiled. "Now, we shall feast."

We entered the inn and sat at a small table in the corner by a fireplace. We ate until our bellies were full and happy. Eating out was completely different in Jack's time. There were no women alone with other women, but instead couples or just men eating for one. It was very strange to see how differently women were treated, and I forgot that women didn't have the same rights then that they did in my time. I wished I could tell some of these people that times would be changing and everyone would be equal eventually.

Back at the hotel, Jack snuck me inside since it was inappropriate for me to be staying with a man. We weren't married, and it was in their eyes trashy, or something like that. They probably thought I was a prostitute. I laughed as we snuck inside and Jack held his laughs in until we got inside the room, then he burst out loud with giggles.

"I must say, you're a sneaky and clever girl, Emmeline Bailey. And I will miss you while you're gone. I wish that I knew when your next arrival would be," he said as we both lay on the bed, staring at each other. I felt his gaze deepen as my smile grew larger. Jack had a power over me that I wish I could will away; it would make leaving so much more bearable.

"I don't know when it will be for you, but it won't be long for me. Time works differently for us, doesn't it?" He nodded. "It could be a week for you, or a month," I explained. "I learned so much from my guide book, but not anything on how to control my visits. I am supposed to be learning as much as I can about your life, but instead I'm disrupting it. You need to go and be with your father, don't you?"

I didn't really know what it was about Jackson Sr. that made Jack want to hide here. I figured it would come up in conversation, but it never did. Jack had always let me talk about my life instead.

He nodded and said, "As much as I'd love to stay here with you, I must return to my father and back into my place."

"Which is?"

"Under his thumb. Like I said before, I don't like the man I could become with my father's guidance."

Hearing this made me sad and I wished I could tell him how it would all end, but even I didn't know what would happen in Jack's future.

"Jack, only you can control what type of man you will be, not your dad or anyone else. You control your fate. And your dad may be well known, like you said before, but you need to do what you want to or else this life is worthless."

He pulled me closer to him and nuzzled into my neck. "I wish it were that easy."

I pulled away and sat up. "It is that easy, Jack. Tell your dad to back off. You might piss him off, but he'll get over it."

He sat up with me and laughed. "If I tell my father to sod off, he may go about and whack me, or worst yet, disown me. I cannot be a man of integrity and own my own shipping company by doing that."

He needed his dad's money and his allies in order to do what he dreamt of. I understood that. I was giving him advice on a topic that I didn't understand. I couldn't very well tell Gram *no* when she asked me to take over her life.

"Well, the next time I see you, Jack, I hope that you're not hiding out."

He took my ring off of the bed side table and handed it to me. His eyes were sad, but he had a smile on his face.

"I guess we shouldn't put it off any longer," he said.

I shook my head and looked down at the ring. I needed to get back, but I didn't want to yet.

"It will be all right, Emmeline. You can go and come back soon, love. I promise I'll be fine. Next time you see me, I'll not be hiding out."

I looked up and grabbed him. I held him so tightly, wishing that the answer would come to me. What was I going to do about these feelings I had for a man in the past? A man in a book that I couldn't properly be with. Could I run away from my life and live inside his world? Would I become a part of history? Would I really be able to live here with him?

"I love you, Jackson Ridgewell," I choked out.

"And I love you, Emmeline Bailey."

I slipped the ring onto my finger and felt the pull instantly. "Until next time," I yelled.

Twenty-Two

I sat upright and looked around my bedroom, searching for signs that I was gone for a long time. Even though I was with Jack for one night, I wasn't sure how long time passed here. I stood up and wobbled as my achy body tried to walk toward the door. I felt like I was hit by a car.

I reached for the handle and pulled the door open when I came face to face with a very distraught Tarryn and Becca.

"Oh my God!" Tarryn said before she grabbed me and pulled me toward her. "I didn't know what to do. You were gone and I...I panicked. I thought you disappeared. Or that you pulled a Jenny. So I called Bec. I had to, Emme. I had no choice."

I pulled her off and willed her to slow down. Her words weren't making any sense. My brain was absolute mush.

"Am I supposed to know what *pulling a Jenny* is? And I'm fine. I'm here, aren't I?"

I gave a laugh, but her sad face didn't respond.

Instead Becca stepped forward with arms folded and said, "She had no choice, Emme."

Oh shit. "Had no choice to do what?"

Now I was freaking out a little.

"I found the book on your bed, open to a page, and I read it...you were in the pages. I didn't know why this time was different," she explained as I shook my head in disbelief. "I didn't understand why you weren't here with me while inside there with him. So I read this."

She held up a book I hadn't seen before.

"I found it inside the hidden room and it was full of information that helped me find out why you weren't back yet. When the first day went by, I realized I couldn't hide you being away any longer." She sighed and threw the book onto my bed. "I was really freaking out, Emme, and I was all alone in this. So I told Becca everything."

I pretty much knew this was what she was going to tell me, but it didn't stop me from throwing my hands up in the air and screaming at her the importance of keeping this a secret. Her face turned red with anger, and she stepped forward and got into my face—totally not what I expected.

"You have no idea how horrible it was dealing with your disappearance, Emme. Everyone was asking questions. People called for you, and on top of that I had to run *your* library, alone. So without Becca here to help me deal, I would have lost my crap, okay? So back off!"

Wow. I knew she was sassy, but this side of Tarryn was not one I wanted to see on a regular basis.

"Tarryn, I'm really sorry for leaving you here to deal with this all alone," I said as I hugged her. "I promise not to ever do it again. I just got into that fight with Rose, and I guess I got lost inside the pages."

"You can say that again," Becca exclaimed.

"It's okay, just don't ever do that without telling me first, okay?" Tarryn asked. Her normal coloring took over and the redness disappeared from her face. "I had to call the Rhode Island library to get some answers, and I have to say, they were very helpful."

"I'd love to hear all about it, but first, can I get some food. I feel horrible." I held my stomach as a hunger unlike anything I'd ever felt before took hold of me.

We sat at Gram's table as Tarryn showed me all the things she found inside the secret room. On the table laid several photographs, more books, and letters. The photographs were of the other Librarians that I had seen before.

"This book has all the information you'll ever need of all the libraries all over the country who are in the sect of The Librarians. That's how I got ahold of the Rhode Island library and talked to Jenny Bailey Hancock's daughter, Ariane," Tarryn explained, as she showed me a photo of Jenny. I recognized her from the photo on the wall.

"Wasn't Jenny the one who decided to stay inside her book?" I asked as I remembered Tarryn telling me her tale before.

She nodded and said, "Yes. Her protector, Beverly, was so distraught that she left the sect and decided never to be part of it again. It can be really damaging when your preserver disappears on you."

I laughed, "I get it!"

I took a bite of spaghetti and sucked the noodle into my mouth as she explained some more.

"Ariane would like to meet us and tell us everything she learned about Jenny and why she got stuck inside her book," Becca chimed in. "She *is* really nice."

Now that we sat at the table together, I felt really happy that Becca was part of our little secret group; I wouldn't have it any other way.

"I'd love to meet her. When can we go?" I asked as I wiped my face clean.

"Let's go tomorrow," Becca suggested. "The library is closed and I have the day off of work, too."

"Road trip!" Tarryn yelled excitedly.

"Whose car are we taking? Because there is no way Gram's beast is going to make that drive," I said. Rhode Island was far, too far for that truck anyway.

"Well, since I'm the only one with a car that's not a hundred years old, that leaves my car," Becca groaned.

"Good, let's leave at first light so that we don't spend the whole day driving, 'kay?"

They both nodded and I excused myself from the table. I needed a shower and my bed. I had just spent the last two days in the wrong time and my body felt sore. I wouldn't be doing that again anytime soon.

As I walked away, the only thoughts that permeated my brain were of Jack and when I would see him again, not going on a road trip with my friends. I had to figure out my life and what direction I wanted to take it. I just didn't know how to do that yet.

Twenty-Three

Normally while driving down I-95, my biggest concern is hitting a moose and either A. Killing myself or B. Killing my car. This time was different; my only thoughts were of Jack. I tried to think of more important things, but he seeped his way into my brain each time. I tried to focus on the radio and a love song came on. I pulled out my phone and began scrolling through photos when I came across the one I had of Jack. I sighed loudly and threw my phone into my open bag.

Tarryn was driving, and Becca had the radio on so loud that the love song was now pounding my skull. I needed to get out of this car, but we had an hour to go still.

"Are you okay back there?" Tarryn asked me from the rear-view mirror.

I nodded, but it was a lie and she knew it. She shut off the radio, thankfully, and pressed me for answers.

"What's really going on?"

How did I explain that I was in love with a guy from the past, who I visited in a book, that I had no future with? I couldn't tell her all my feelings because even I didn't know what was going on inside my head.

"I am just confused about Jack and, well, my task really. Remember when you asked me if I was falling in love with him?"

She nodded.

"Well, I am. And I've never been in love before. I just don't know what to do about my situation. I want nothing more than to be with him, but on the other hand, I don't know him that well. I've never met his family and I've never spent more than one night with him. How do I give up my life, for that?"

Tarryn squealed and Becca yelped. "You're going to live with him?" Becca asked in shock.

I rolled my eyes because that's not what I said.

"He asked me to, but I don't think I can. Then again, I didn't think I could run a library either. You guys don't get it," I sighed. "I've never been in love *or* had a serious boyfriend. The way Jack makes me feel is special to me. I can't decide what to do about it or him."

Becca nodded and her face calmed a bit more.

"You need to do what your heart tells you, Emme," Becca began. "I tried to give this one love advice and it didn't go so well." She pointed her thumb toward Tarryn, who snorted.

"Take it from me, Emme, once you find love, don't let go. But if it means giving up your life to be with him, it isn't worth it," Tarryn said as she stared out the window. "I gave up a lot for my ex. Even my own self-worth. He ended up treating me like dirt and left me feeling worthless and unloved."

For the rest of the drive I thought about what Tarryn had said. I would have to give up my life to be with Jack. I would have to leave my whole world to join his, and I wasn't sure I was ready to do that. I would be joining a time where women had basically no rights to anything and no voices either. I couldn't handle not being able to be myself in a time where a girl like me was an oddity.

I loved him, but did love mean giving up everything?

****

The small library just outside of Providence, Rhode Island, sat back from the street and was surrounded by large trees. We had arrived early enough to meet with Ariane, but I was tired as if it were night. I sipped my coffee as we walked into the library, and I suddenly felt nervous.

Jenny Bailey Hancock had left her life behind, including her own daughter, and I was about to learn why. Somehow I felt like this day would either make or break my future with Jack.

A petite woman sat at the desk, and I knew right away it wasn't Jenny's daughter. I remembered Jenny from the photograph, and this woman was not related. She greeted us politely and Tarryn told her who we were here to see. While we waited I meandered over to a large glass case where pictures were pinned. I noticed Jenny's face right away. She was standing with a baby in her arms and her curly light blonde hair was pinned to her head fashionably.

"I love that photo of her, but I can't say that I remember her like that at all." I turned around and knew that this woman was Ariane.

"How do you remember her then?" I asked.

She sighed. "Gone. I remember that she left me a lot, and then one day, she didn't come back."

Ariane was older than I thought she would be with curling white hair and soft wrinkles that spread along her face.

"I'd love to tell you about my mother, Miss Bailey. We are family after all." That was true, but I didn't feel right calling this woman, I hardly knew, family. "Follow me into the meeting room and we can talk about everything."

We followed Ariane down a small staircase and into a bright room that held several bookcases full of books. She tapped a button on the wall and the bookcase that was there opened to another set of stairs. This library had a secret room just like mine did. We followed her in silence as we descended into a dark room. My heart pounded in anticipation of what was to come next when a light came on. The room was a lot like Gram's, with the photographs of Librarians and books that no doubt they'd traveled in.

"Have a seat, ladies. Would anyone like tea or coffee?" Ariane asked.

"I think we just want to get some answers about how Jenny disappeared." I spoke for all of us.

We sat at a large stone table, and Ariane sat down slowly with a grunt.

"It's not as easy getting down here these days. It used to be easier when I was younger. I used to follow my mother down here when I was a toddler, and she would let me play in here when I got a little older," she said, her eyes downcast. "Then one day she told me about who we were: The Bailey women. She told me the importance of our tasks and that I would be able to travel and preserve just like her. But I never was taught how because she left me too soon."

I wondered if Ariane ever got over this fact or if she thought about her mom every day. I used to think about mine all the time and then one day I just stopped. I didn't cry anymore and I didn't wish for her to come back either.

I wasn't going to change the fact that she died, no matter how much I cried or wished. But disappearing was harder, I supposed. You never knew where they were, not exactly.

"What about Beverly? Didn't she try to teach you?" Becca asked.

Ariane shook her head. "Sadly, no. Beverly didn't take my mother's disappearance well. She died about a year after she left us."

The whole room went still. I suppose that a protector really was linked to the traveler, and now I understood how scared Tarryn was when I didn't come back. It made me feel awful.

Ariane looked at me then and her eyes got very serious.

"Emmeline," she began, "you are a visitor in his life and you've been given a huge responsibility to preserve his book, not to have a relationship with him."

I shook my head confused on several levels. How did she even know about Jack at all?

"How do you know that I'm having a relationship with him?" I asked.

"I can see it in your eyes—the look of love. And your friends told me over the phone, but do not be mad at them. You have to see that a relationship of this magnitude could ultimately damage not only your life but his."

I couldn't see how I would be damaging Jack's life in any way.

Sure her mom left her, but I didn't have a child to leave behind. I wouldn't be hurting myself in any way other than leaving what I knew and loved behind. But when I thought about what I had here in this time, I knew that if I left it all would be okay. If anything, I would be the one who would have to adjust to the harsh time of Jack's life. Besides, I never set anything into motion about leaving this world for Jack's. All I knew at that moment was I loved him and we couldn't be together like I wanted.

"My mother was married to my father for many years, but over time I suppose the romance faded. My mother had a job to preserve books that had come in from a colleague of hers overseas. She took to the task right away, and I was with my father most of the time. He didn't know what Mother was doing; he thought she was only preserving old books, not the actual history inside them. She was one of the first to form The Librarians along with her cousin, Grace Bailey."

My great-grandmother.

"Grace and Jenny formed a tight bond and soon began visiting one another inside the stories themselves; they would read about similar historians at the same time. I don't exactly know how they did it, but they loved what they did."

Ariane took a drink of water and settled into her chair. I sat back and realized I was biting my fingernails in anticipation.

"For a while, this appeased her and she didn't really mind that my father was gone while she was tending to me. But when I was ten, that all changed. Grace Bailey sent a package to my mother, and I remember that I was sent upstairs to my room to play while she worked. She did her job, and when I was called down for dinner, she seemed happy. Happier and more delightful than I had ever seen her."

I gasped. "She met someone inside the pages, didn't she?"

She nodded solemnly. "Indeed, she did. Alberto Ruiz was an explorer from Spain, and my mother fell in love with him from page one. She started traveling without Beverly, and I'll never forget the last time they spoke. They had a huge argument over him and my mother told Beverly to leave. Before she left, Beverly warned Jenny that she was going to regret leaving this world for his. That not only would it hurt me and my father, but that it would alter his future and he would never be known as an explorer. His future would change upon the arrival of my mother into his life, and this would damage the world around him and her. I didn't understand until after my mother left me. I couldn't comprehend the warning then."

I was sitting at the edge of my seat, curious about the warning as well. I bit my cheek dying to hear what happened to Jenny.

"Well, what happened?" I blurted.

"My father searched for her for years after she left, but I knew where she was. And when I was twelve years old, we learned about the Spanish explorers in our history books. I wondered what I would learn about Alberto Ruiz and if I would see or hear about my mother as well. It was the only connection I had to her now that she had left me.

"When my history teacher taught us all there was to learn, I asked him one day after class about Alberto, and he told me that there was never a Spanish explorer by that name. I thought maybe he was wrong, so I took my search to the local library where I learned the fate of Alberto Ruiz. After my mother joined him in the book, she had altered his life so dramatically that he never became the amazing historian and explorer he was meant to be. I found out by books and by meeting with a fellow Librarian of our sect that she had swayed his path just enough that he never became the great man he was supposed to be."

She leaned closer to me and took my hands in hers. Her soft skin reminded me of Gram, but nothing could calm my pounding heart at that moment. Hearing what Jenny had done to Alberto's life made everything different. I could see now the life-altering effects of what Jenny had done and of what I could have done if I didn't come back from the last trip.

"Emme," she began, "your job is to preserve his story, a story already set in motion. You go into his books at the most pivotal points in his life. Times when he is making amazing changes that could impact who he becomes in the end."

I thought about all the times I entered the book and saw Jack.

Having his goodbye party; right before he left for America; boarding the ship; his arrival in Maine. All times that would be important in shaping who Jack was to become, and I could have ruined it for him. Suddenly, I thought of the things I said to him about being his own man and not letting his father run his life for him. And also about the times I kissed him and when it was more than kissing. Could I have ruined the person Jack became by doing those things? I was just there to observe and report, not to fall in love.

An idea popped into my head in hopes that it wasn't too late.

"He's already famous, isn't he? How would I change his future if it's already happened?"

That was the most confusing part of this whole journey I was on. Thinking about it literally gave me a headache.

"Harold Lockhart explained it best in his fourth guide book," she said, before pulling out the book and placing it into my hands. "He explains that even if it's already happened, the past isn't fixed. Nothing is set into stone. A preserver can alter the future because how would we, in the present, even know if something changed? We only know what we remember and if the past is changed. If a historian's life is wiped-out, then that alters our memory as well."

My head swam at just the thought of such a thing occurring. I could have screwed up his life and never knew it.

"Yeah, like if you went back and stopped my birth, how would you know I was ever alive?" Tarryn said to Becca, who laughed.

"Sometimes I wish I could change such things," Becca teased.

"The most important thing to remember is that you are there to record and to learn. Do not alter his life in any way, Emme. It's normal to have feelings for him, but you mustn't let those feelings change his course. Nothing should stop him from becoming the man he is to be," Ariane said finally.

I took her warning, and I wouldn't forget it. I stood up from the chair on wobbly legs and shook her hand.

"Thank you," I mumbled. "I think we should be going back now. It's getting late."

And before I could hear any argument, I left.

Twenty-Four

Two days had passed since we met with Ariane. I regretted how I left that day, but the emotions of the moment were hindering my manners. I would have normally not been such an ass, but what could I say? I was in shock.

As the days went by, I couldn't even look at Jack's books; I was too scared. I could ruin his life if I went back. My plan was to get my head right and go back when I didn't feel the way I did about him. If I waited a month, then so be it. I'd start dating and maybe I'd find a distraction. Then I'd be able to go back and I could actually do my job right.

I read Harold's book and found it quite boring, if not tiring. But there were a few times I didn't fall asleep. Learning that the future can change rapidly and so could the past. I did have a duty to the sect of Librarians and I would uphold it. I promised Gram and I don't go back on promises. Except that I promised Jack I would be back to see him soon, and I wouldn't be upholding that one.

****

The summer months went by like the breeze on the shore and, in all that time, no distractions were found. The guys in this town were either not available or not attractive. I couldn't find a guy in Bay Ridge nor any town close to it. And I wasn't settling for an *okay* guy either. He would have to be just as attractive as Jack for it to work.

Every time I fell asleep I saw Jack's face just before drifting off. Needless to say, I wasn't sleeping well lately. I was on my third cup of coffee in the secret room, looking over old photos of Librarians. I had discovered many secrets about the women in our sect, places they had seen and people they had learned about. It was the only way for me to keep my mind busy since finding a guy wasn't working out. I found that spending time reading about the women who preceded me as a Librarian kept me on track, for now. The phone rang, pulling me away from the room.

"Bay Ridge Library," I answered in a sleepy voice.

"Emme?"

It was Rose. I sighed. I was too tired to talk to Rose about anything, especially our fight.

"Yeah, Rose. What's up?"

I wasn't intending to be so brash, but dang, I was tired. If I wasn't, I would have been happy to hear her voice. Truth be told, I didn't even think about our fight; I had other more important things on my mind.

"I called to see if we could meet up and talk," she asked, sounding desperate.

I yawned. "Yeah, sure. When?"

There was a pause and soon after she said, "Um...is now okay?"

Now? Really? I wanted nothing more than to shut off all

the lights and drag my tired ass up the stairs to my bed. It was calling me as we spoke.

"Okay. Where?" I gave in.

"Well, there is this old bank building up on the hill. Can we meet there?"

She wanted to talk to me and she wanted to meet at a bank? Weird place for a long talk about friendship, but whatever. I was too tired to argue.

We said goodbye and I closed up the library. Tarryn was off doing who knows what, so I locked up and headed to the bank. The sun was beginning to lower in the sky, leaving a beautiful glow over our town. It was times like these that made me love Maine so much. Nothing was prettier than fall on the East Coast. I loved the summer but there was something so cozy about autumn.

Autumn meant apple cider and pumpkin pie. And it also meant my first Thanksgiving without Gram.

I didn't even know what I was going to do without her this year. And the thought of Christmas without her was even worse.

I liked to think that I was doing pretty well for myself after her loss. I was independent and running the library like she wished. But hosting dinners and celebrating without her by my side was not going to be easy.

It dawned on me then that maybe running away to be with Jack would be easier than dealing with life without her. I couldn't keep walking away from my life though; I had to stay and live it.

I pulled into the old bank building and saw Rose's car parked in the lot. I swung the truck into a space and shut off the engine. The windows were down and a gush of ocean breeze blew through the cab. It felt amazing, and it reminded me of Jack and the time we played in the ocean water together. Life was never going to be easy and many things would remind me of him. I couldn't deny that he had made a huge impression in my world; he made me fall in love for the first time. There was never going to be a first time for that again.

"Emme!" Rose called out to me and waved.

I waved back and got out of the truck. She sat down at a small bench overlooking the beautiful ocean below us.

"I have to ask," I said as I sat down next to her. "Why are we meeting here?"

She laughed. "Well, it's this building that made me realize what an ass I was the last time we saw each other. I was here making a deposit when I saw the sign on the building."

She pointed to the brass sign that I couldn't read from where we stood, by the door.

"It said how long this building has been standing in Bay Ridge. This bank was built in the early 1900s, and it survived the Great Depression. It's a landmark, Emme.

"I was a total bitch to you, Emme. I shouldn't have said those things to you. It's not your fault that you left. The truth is," she paused. "The truth is, I'm jealous you got to leave and go to California."

I laughed. "It was only for a year, Rose. Look where I'm sitting now. I'm back in the same town I desperately tried to get away from all my life. I run a library. I'm not a doctor."

She smiled bashfully. "I am a doctor, but I'm a broke doctor who's stuck with student loans. I really want my own office, but I realized that if tearing down your Gram's place was the only way for me to do that, then I was going about it wrong."

I put my arm around her and gave her a hug. I was

thankful she understood the importance of keeping the library where it was. "Rose, we are going to get you your own office. You don't need to worry about that."

Rose had been my friend for a long time. She may have been a lot older than me, but she always treated me like an equal. She was a true friend, and I needed her in my life just as much as she needed me.

We sat at the bench talking until sundown. She had an early day and I needed my bed. We hugged goodbye, and I vowed to help her find a way to get her own place.

"Bye, Emme. See you soon, okay?"

I nodded and waved to her as she drove away.

As I walked to the truck, I passed by the bank. It survived the Great Depression and that was pretty incredible. Any building that survived such a time was amazing. The brick front looked like it had been re-done a few times, but the foundation was strong.

The two-story building had a lot of history, and I bet it was beautiful in its time. I wished I could have seen it when it was first built.

The brass sign on the front that Rose had told me about looked like it needed a good polish as I looked closer to read it.

When I did, I felt faint. My whole body began to shake. I wasn't just standing at the site of history, I was standing at the site of Jackson Ridgewell Jr.'s history.

Twenty-Five

The sign read:
This site is dedicated to the founder of Bay Ridge and the founder of Ridgewell Banking: Jackson Ridgewell Jr.

Built in 1901, Ridgewell Bank stood strong against the storm of the Great Depression. It is in the memory of the people of Bay Ridge that this site be declared Historic.

Jack. My Jack.

He founded Bay Ridge and he founded a bank. A big bank, from the looks of it.

I swayed on my feet and almost fell on my butt, if not for a tree beside me.

I had to get back to the library and I had to see him.

I rushed inside and didn't even say anything to Tarryn as she greeted me. I grabbed the book and showed it to her, so she knew what I was doing, and then plopped down on the couch and started reading.

I blinked and whooshed. Instantly I was standing in front of a big beautiful home. It looked a lot like this old house in

Bay Ridge that had become some sort of attraction years ago. But it couldn't be the same. Most of the old houses looked alike in Bay Ridge.

I was standing there watching the house, just waiting for someone to come out of it or to see some movement. I wasn't going to knock on the door. Again, I was wearing clothes not of this era, and I wouldn't know what to say anyway.

"Hi, is Jack home? I'm his ..." What was I to him anyway? His girlfriend? His lover? His secret?

I heard yelling coming from behind the house and I decided that walking along the tree line to check it out would be the best way to do so.

I skimmed the trees and walked slowly. It was, thankfully, cooler outside, which meant one of two things: years had passed or only a few months. The summer heat was gone and I recognized the autumn weather immediately. I stopped dead in my tracks when I saw a man walking outside of the home.

"Argus! Come here you mangy mutt!"

It was Jack. He looked different; older perhaps or maybe he only grew in a beard. His full beard covered the face that I loved so much, but I was okay with that.

He put his hands in his pockets and sighed deeply.

I held my breath, wishing that he would just look my way and see me standing here staring at him like a stalker.

Come on, Jack. See me.

At that moment he looked my way, and I froze. Maybe him seeing me wasn't the best idea. I did still love him, despite trying to stay away.

My feelings for him I couldn't deny. Thinking I could just hide from him until I went back wasn't a great idea though, since I was here and I was supposed to be recording pivotal moments in his life. I sincerely doubted calling for a dog was life changing though.

His eyes scanned the trees and at once they stopped, on me.

"Who's there?" he called out.

Shit.

He walked down the steps of his house and began walking toward me at a fast pace. I backed up and hit a tree with my back. This wasn't a great idea. What if he didn't remember me? Maybe many years had passed and he was married now with a litter of kids.

He stopped at the tree line and his eyes grew wide.

"Emmeline," he whispered. "You're here."

He ran to me then and took me in his arms. I fell into him despite my warnings of falling further in love with him. He landed a kiss on my mouth that made all thoughts disappear.

I could taste the desperation in his lips as his kisses became deeper. He didn't hold back as he lifted me up against the tree. I wrapped my legs around his torso, pulling him closer to me.

We were electric. I couldn't deny the way he made my skin feel like fire when he touched me. He began kissing my neck and throat and down to my chest.

Then he looked at me and that sexy look of his disappeared as he said, "Where have you been?"

The sadness in his eyes gutted me.

"Jack," I said as I kissed him. "I'm so sorry that I wasn't here earlier. I wish...I wish it could be controlled," I choked out.

Before I knew it, I was crying and kissing him again.

My salty tears ran down my face and into our embrace. He pulled back and with that same look asked, "Why are you sad?"

"Because I've missed you. And I hate that I caused you pain, Jack."

He let me down, gently. And put a distance between us which made me feel empty and bare.

"I only wondered where you were for the past year, Emmeline."

I swallowed hard. *A year?*

"I looked for you, everywhere I went. I waited for you. Dammit, I'm still waiting for you and you're bloody right in front of me." He raked his hands through his hair. "I can't do this."

His words flew at me like knives, piercing my heart over and over again.

"I can't come when I want to, Jack. It doesn't work like that. That's what makes our relationship so complicated." I wished I had the words to heal his hurt, but I didn't.

"Relationship? This isn't anything like that Emmeline. You have to be present to be with me properly. Please explain to me how it works."

"I'm here to observe you, Jack, you know that. You're becoming someone so important, and I am only to come to you when you're actually making history. *Your* history. I have absolutely no control over where the book will take me."

He shook his head in confusion.

"So you can only come to me when I'm preforming something important?" He was catching on quickly but growing more irritated.

"Yes. The book only allows me to travel here at certain points in your life. Otherwise I would have been here sooner. I never wanted to leave you in the first place," I said, truthfully.

He turned away from me, rigidly.

"Then why did you leave me, Emmeline? Why didn't you stay? You didn't have to take on the role as observer. You could have stayed with me forever."

I reached for him and took his hand in mine, surprised he let me.

"You know that I needed to leave that day. You had to go meet your father and I had a life to get back to."

I hated that he was so agitated, and I hated that so much time had passed.

He turned toward me and nodded.

"Yes, I had responsibilities. Emmeline, you could have come with me, and you know that you could have walked away from your life. You even told me it wasn't what you wanted to be doing. A whole year has passed me by, and I'm not the boy I was then. I've become a man with great purpose in this town," he said. "I hate to put it so frank, but I had to live my life."

I nodded. I wished that he would have told me that before he kissed me like he did. Before he threw me against the tree and made my blood heat with passion.

"I live here in this home, and I looked for you daily. But you never arrived." He searched my face and ran his fingers across my cheeks. "I yearn for you at night when I'm alone. Emmeline, why is it that you haunt me so? Why can't I turn away from you and leave you standing here alone? It's what you deserve."

I took a deep, painful breath in. "Is that what you want to do, Jack? You want to leave me here alone?"

If that was his wish, then I would walk away. I would wait until I could go back home and I'd never come back, if it meant sparing him the pain I saw in his eyes.

"I can leave, Jack. I know what you will become and

what you will do, and I can tell you now that I'm so proud of you. I'm proud that I knew you. I think it would be best if I stopped coming to you."

He looked down and slowly back up at me again.

"No."

"No?" I asked curiously.

"No, I don't want you to walk away," he replied, as he swept me up into his arms. "I want you to stay, for now. There is something I want you to see."

He carried me through the woods, not to his home, but somewhere farther away. Finally, he put my feet down when we approached a cliff overlooking the ocean below. To the right, in the distance was a building that looked familiar.

"I brought you here to show you what I am doing with my life," he said as he stared out toward the waves.

He sighed, preparing himself.

"While you were gone, I have done much thinking about my life. I finally freed myself from my father's clutches, but in doing so, I fear that I caused him so much pain. Pain I never intended to cause."

He didn't meet my eyes, no matter how hard I tried to get him to. Instead he kept his face outward and away from me.

He deserved to be angry with me. I was just thrown for a loop by his forwardness upon seeing me and now he pushed me away. I was beyond confused. Did he want me here or not?

He said he did, but I didn't feel welcome. He was almost cold and calculated in his actions now, not the same Jack from a year ago, that was for sure.

"My father suffered a heart attack shortly after I told him my plans for the future, the plans that I was going to become a man who made a difference, but without him. It seems fate gave me what I asked for, because he is gone."

"Oh, Jack. I'm so sorry." I felt instantly awful for him. "I too suffered the loss of my parents and my Gram. I never wished that for you."

He finally turned toward me and met my gaze.

"You never talk much about your life, Emmeline. I never knew you lost so many. I suppose there is much we both do not know about one another besides *lust* and *infatuation*. Because that's all we had between the two of us, you know?"

His words instantly gutted me, but I tried hard not to show my pain. My face remained stone even though inside I was breaking to pieces.

He never truly loved me. He was just merely infatuated with me. I was only a girl he thought he loved. The one time fling. The girl who took his virginity and made him see pleasure for one night. I was not the love of his life.

I was the fool then.

That was okay. I would play the fool if it meant that Jack would live the life he was meant to, if I didn't disrupt his life like Jenny disrupted her lover's. I would never wipe Jack out of existence no matter how much I wanted to beg him to tell me he loved me.

I loved him too much to ruin his life. I wouldn't be selfish. I was selfish before when I left my life behind and moved to California. I left Gram when I should have stayed to take care of her. Maybe her life would have been longer if I stayed. I could have gotten my degree at home. It was my own personal need to be free that left her alone.

I wouldn't do that to Jack.

"So then, why are we here?" I choked out.

"I wanted to show you that," he said pointing to the

building. "It is the future home of Ridgewell Bank and Loan. I have secured my future, Emmeline."

His bank. That is why the building looked so familiar.

"I have seen that building before, Jack," I told him, wide eyed. "I just saw it today, and that is why I decided to open the book. I knew I had to see you, to tell you how much you made a difference. Jack, the building is still standing."

He shook his head in disbelief. "You saw it?"

He looked almost like a kid on Christmas. He was suddenly so happy that it threw me. He had gone from angry to delightful in the matter of seconds.

"I read that the bank and loan opens in a few years, and it survives a tumultuous time."

I had hoped that that would bring another smile to his face, but it didn't. He just nodded like I gave him the weather forecast. His happy mood declined.

"Well, then. I suppose I will reach my goal. I am going to do what I set out to do then. Good."

I was so happy for him. He was going to get all that he desired and do it all without his father's help.

"I want you to know that you didn't kill your father, Jack. He did not die because of you."

His eyes met mine and he looked almost empty inside. I suppose that was what was wrong with him; he was devoid of emotion.

"Doesn't matter now anyway. You cannot bring back the dead. My mother lives with me. She's very happy to help me in my ventures. And I have a dog, but I cannot find him, presently."

I remembered him calling out for the dog.

"Argus?"

He nodded.

"My house is not as I wish it to be yet. It's not the estate I plan to build, but once the bank and loan opens, it will be. I will send for all of my staff back home to join me here."

His house was beautiful, an estate was what came to mind when I looked at it. It was as large as his home was in England. I wanted to tell him that he would become the founder of the town and it was the very town I lived in currently, but I didn't dare make this about me.

"Your home is simply perfect, Jack."

He shook his head and looked away again.

I was losing him. I felt it in my bones. He wasn't the same warm, happy Jack. That Jack was gone now and in his place was a man who had focused on making a name for himself and becoming someone worthy of his father's love, even if his father was gone.

"So you do not have to come and study me anymore. I am no longer your subject."

I froze. "Study you?"

"Yes, this coming here and haunting me. You can stop now. I do not need you," he said with venom. It was as harsh as someone who was shooing away a stray animal, trying to get it to leave and stay gone forever.

"Jack, don't say that. We can still be friends, can't we? I mean, you just held me in your arms and kissed me. Surely—"

"Surely, what, Emmeline? You think I have feelings for you?"

"Jack, please don't. You already explained that I was just an infatuation to you. I don't need to hear anything else."

My head began to spin, but I fought the urge to leave like this. The tugging felt faster and more rapid.

"I only kissed you because I was confused. That's what you do to me, Emmeline. You confuse me into thinking that you care about me. Then you leave me. I am going to live my life without you, Emmeline. And you're never to come back here, understand?"

My heart broke into a million pieces; I could feel it in my chest as it exploded. The pull from my time was darkening Jack's face, and I knew I only had seconds left. I wanted to stay and work this out, but I couldn't.

"I won't bother you again, Jack. Goodbye."

Twenty-Six

I fell upon my bed dry heaving. I felt Tarryn's arms around me, but I was numb to anything else. She had helped me into bathroom as I threw up the contents in my stomach until I couldn't any more. She ran her fingers over my hair and began to start a bath for me. I undressed, not caring that she would see me. I was in so much pain that nothing mattered.

"You were fighting the pull of time, Emme. You should have come back when you felt the first tug," she said as she helped me get into the bath. "You were thrashing around on the bed, and at first I thought you were having a seizure. You scared me."

I lay into the steamy hot water. "Sorry." I couldn't form larger sentences, so I hoped that would be enough.

"It's all right. You look like shit, Emme. Do you want to go to the hospital?" She felt my forehead and clucked her tongue.

"No. I just want to lie here until the feeling passes."

Tears ran down my face, and I let them come until I was dry heaving again.

"Emme, you're freaking me out. What happened?"

Seeing Tarryn's face and her concern for me made me tell her everything that happened, despite the lack of energy. I started with the phone call from Rose and ended at the dreadfully awful incident with Jack. That was what I would be calling it from now on. The incident where I left my broken heart in Jack's time.

"He was awful, Tar. He is so different. How can a person change that much in a year's time?" I whispered.

She shook her head. "I only know I have been there before. I recognize that look, that feeling. It's something I can tell you I don't ever want to feel again."

I sank into the water, wanting to drown.

I would never be happy again. I hated this life and wanted to leave this place. It was him. This whole town was Jack. It was his history, and I would never escape it.

I knew what I needed to do. I wouldn't tell Tarryn yet. She would talk me out of it, and I would never follow through with it.

"You know he didn't mean what he said to you," Tarryn tried. "He is probably just saying that to you to protect himself."

I sighed. "Maybe, so. But you weren't there to see his face. The anger was written all over it."

Maybe he was just trying to protect his heart. I'll never know because I'll never go back.

I had plans and I had to get started on them right away.

****

Over the next few weeks I made preparations to leave the whole library and all the books inside of it, including the ones belonging to The Librarians, to Tarryn. It didn't feel strange at all to leave everything to a person I hadn't known for very long. Tarryn was my protector, and as such, she was trusted beyond compare.

I was finished with school and passed my exams with flying colors. I wasn't surprised since I had nothing but school to focus on. There was no Jack anymore and no traveling either.

Tarryn was doing great running the library on her own. I told her that I needed time to heal, and she took the reins under the pretense that I was taking a break.

Rose would be fine because she had a solid idea to build her own office and to take hold of her career.

Becca was busy with her coffee shop and started dating a new guy. I honestly do not know where she found him because he was great to her. But being around them in their happiness made me a bitter person, and I wasn't happy about that.

So I took my time and I buried myself in the prospects of moving to England. I searched for a job and awaited a response. It wouldn't take long to find something for work while I made plans for leaving.

Sure I was running away again, but there was nothing left for me here. Every part of Maine reminded me of Jack, and that simply would not do. Besides, I was young and I needed to act my age a little bit. I had lost myself somewhere along the line, and I wanted to find her again. I wanted to be a little reckless and a little less responsible. I wanted to go to nightclubs and party. I wanted to kiss boys and not have to get their phone number after. I wanted to be young.

I wanted to see beautiful things again, outside of this town. I had run away before, and I would survive it now, like

I had then.

I was taking care of my end of that bargain. The books were going to a fellow preserver just outside of Northern Maine. She agreed to take over my books and preserve them since I couldn't. I would never again time-travel, nor would I be part of The Librarians. Once I did this, I was done.

It was late one Friday night that I stepped inside the hidden room to take inventory. It was important that I do this so I knew exactly how many books were done and how many still needed attending for the library up north.

Lockhart said in his book that once a book has been preserved, the Librarian was to seal it with wax along the outside of it. Whoever had done so with these books has pressed Gram's ring into it as proof that it was done.

There weren't many books that still needed to be preserved, but just enough to keep the new girl busy.

I sat down in the chair with a thump and looked around the room. All The Librarians stared back at me from their photos. Guilt overcame me for the first time since this decision. I had been feeling so confident that I was doing the right thing up until then. These women were not doing me any favors.

I hadn't told any of my friends what I was planning, yet. They simply wouldn't understand. It was easy to think that owning my own library was fun, but they didn't comprehend what pain it had caused me. I wouldn't be a Jenny; I wouldn't go into the book and hurt Jack's future all for my own selfish feelings. And I wasn't going to be like Grace and treat my duty as a simple job that needed to be done. For me it was something magical, and it should be done by someone who would respect it and cherish it. I always saw it as a burden *and* a blessing. I couldn't see it as just one without the other.

It brought me into Jack's life, and as amazing as that had been, look how it ended. Jack hated me, and I was hurting more than I have ever before. This was like a death. It felt the same as it did when Gram died. The only difference this time was that Gram was really gone forever. Jack, however, was reachable by book at any time, but he didn't want me around.

No matter how much I thought about it, I always arrived at the same point; Jack asked me not to come back. How could I go back without him knowing? I stuck out like a sore-thumb.

So the choice to throw in the towel was simple.

"Hello? Is there anyone here?"

I jumped at the sound of a man's voice coming from the library. Surely I had locked the doors. How did he get in here?

I looked at the time, six o'clock. We had been closed for an hour.

"Be right with you," I called out, before shutting off the lights and picking up my papers. I exited the room and tried to compose myself. I wasn't prepared to help anyone check out books, and I simply felt irritated to have to do so.

"We're closed," I said as I approached the man. He had his back to me as he ran his fingers over the books in the new arrivals section.

"I won't be long. I'm just looking for something new to read this weekend," he said, with an air of confidence.

He did hear me say we were closed, right?

"We are closed, sir. You can come back Monday and check out a book. I shut down the computers an hour ago."

It was stupid of me to not properly lock the doors, but closed was closed.

I checked the sign, and it was indeed flipped. At least I did that right.

"I really need a book," he called out to me. "I won't be long. I just want to get something real quick and then I'll leave. Surely, you will understand, right? You know when you need a good book, you just can't wait to get it in your hands. It's like a drug."

Would I understand? Yeah, I understood he was an ass who probably was used to getting his way. Looking at how he was dressed told me he had money. He wore dark denim jeans that looked freshly ironed and a pressed blue shirt. No one in this town dressed that nicely, especially to go to the library.

"Look, I meant what I said. We are closed. And you gotta leave," I said, firmly. "Sorry, but I have plans."

He turned around, chuckling at me as he did. He had looked over the new arrivals and chose a teen romance. I tried to read the title, but his hands blocked it from view.

"I just want to get this one book, and oh...if you have a copy of the dictionary too, please," he said completely serious.

The dictionary? This guy was severely strange.

"Look, I said no. We are closed, and if you don't—" I didn't finished my sarcastic comment because my eyes landed on his face. My breath caught and my body froze.

His smile reached his blue eyes and he stood there waiting for me to go on, but I couldn't.

"If I don't, what?" he asked, as he leaned forward on the counter, bringing that familiar face just a little closer.

Surely, I wasn't seeing this correctly. Was I going mad? I must have been because when I looked at this stranger I saw a face I knew so well.

No. That wasn't it, because when I blinked my eyes and pinched myself, I still saw the face I had grown to love and know so well. It was the face of Jackson Ridgewell Jr.

Twenty-Seven

"**W**ell? Can I get this book or not?" he asked teasingly.

My mind willed me to speak, but my mouth wasn't cooperating. I just nodded and took the book and scanned it. The beep didn't sound like normal, so I looked down. Duh, the computers weren't up, because we were freaking closed!

I just handed him the book, all while staring at him like a freak would. Was he Jack? Did he find a way to come to me? Was he just playing with me until I said something to him?

I was too scared I was going crazy to ask him anything. Besides, my question would scare him off, and I'd get no answers. I could see it now. *"Excuse me, do you know you look like a guy I know. He lives in the past and I time-travel to see him."* Yeah, that won't go over well.

So, I decided to be silent.

"And, my dictionary?"

I shook my head. What was up with this guy and his need for a dictionary?

"Why? Why do you need that?" I asked, giving in.

He laughed a throaty laugh that was nothing like Jack's. In fact he sounded nothing like Jack, but his voice was familiar. He may look just like my Jack, but he wasn't him. I wasn't sure how I knew then, but I did.

"I was told I needed to study it," he said simply.

I shook my head slowly again, trying to clear my blurry and frazzled brain.

"How do I know you?" I dared to ask. It was the only thing I could ask that would give me some idea as to why he looked like Jack's twin.

"We have yet to meet in person, but we've talked on the phone many times, Miss. Bailey," he said as he stuck his hand out in front of me to shake. I looked down at it and back at his face.

No. Just no.

This was the guy from JR Builders: Jason something. The asshole who wanted to rip down the very building he was standing in.

At that moment my mind was reeling. I was going through many emotions, but the biggest one was shock because I realized that Jason, the phone stalker, was related to Jack.

Our last phone conversation, if you would call it that, he told me that his great-great-grandfather founded Bay Ridge. At the time I couldn't put two and two together, but now I knew. I had found out that Jack was the founder and he was the one who made our town what it was, and this jerk-wad in front of me was tearing down Jack's memory.

He might as well be stomping on his grave. He was ruining everything that Jack did to become who he was and that made me angry.

"You have some nerve coming in here, you know that?" It was a rhetorical question, of course, but he answered anyway.

"I didn't know that, actually. But you seem to like telling me things that I don't know about myself. Please do continue; I love learning new things," he said with a smirk.

This guy was nothing like Jack. He may have his face and be his freaking doppelganger, but he was classless.

"You came in here just to be an ass, didn't you? Wait, do not answer that," I spat. "You aren't quite sure what ass means yet." I handed him the dictionary on my desk and it landed with a thump on the counter in front of him. "You can get the hell out of *my* library now."

He didn't leave. He didn't apologize. No, this guy laughed. He laughed at *me*. It was time to give him a full lesson on how awful he was for trying to take all that was left of my past.

"You could have been doing good things, but you're ruining the history of our town. And I will never sell to you or your company, Mr. Whatever-your-name-is. So you can go now, and you can bet that I will not let you tear down one more building in this this town."

They were just words that I said. Idle threats to a man who needed to hear them at the time. I wasn't going to be able to follow through with them when all I was planning on doing was running away from this town anyway.

How could I stop him when I wouldn't even be here?

"My name is Mr. Ridgewell. Jason Ridgewell."

"Wait, what?" I asked, as I shook my head.

He leaned closer, his scent drifting my way. He smelled good, like the damn Devil, and I fought my attraction to him. He was cute, but that was because he wore the face of the guy I was in love with.

I shook my head and cleared my thoughts. "Well, Mr. Ridgewell, tell me how you are honoring your family's name by tearing down my library? Jack would be so disappointed in what you were doing to his dream."

His cocky grin faded and he pushed off of the counter. His face turned confused.

"How did you know that name?"

Oh shit. I was in hot water now. Why did I have to be so short tempered? I was never going to explain this correctly.

"Uh...I'm a college student," I said, like it made sense—it didn't. I mentally smacked myself. Not my finest moment, and he was witnessing the whole thing.

"Uh-huh."

"And I'm studying the history of Bay Ridge, for a paper." My excuse was so lame that I almost felt ashamed. I couldn't very well tell him I knew Jack. I needed to deflect fast. "That doesn't matter anyway," I started. "Why are you so intent on taking this place?"

This douche-nozzle was a Ridgewell and he wanted my Gram's property. He wanted to tear down the very library that allowed me to see Jack and learn about his importance in history, and I couldn't even explain it to him. He wouldn't understand nor did he deserve to hear it.

He chuckled again, and I wanted to slap him. He had a habit of making me feel like an idiot, and I just met him. He must be a delightful person to be around.

"You don't have many friends, do you, Jason?"

He stopped laughing, like I struck a chord. "What makes you say that?"

I got him right where it hurt.

"I can tell that a guy like you is lonely, because firstly, you call me a lot, which indicates you make your work your life. And most people like that do not have time for friends. Secondly, you're here on a Friday evening, when most people are out somewhere more exciting. You are one lonely guy."

I uncrossed my arms and took the teen book he had put on the counter and put it back onto the shelf. I could feel his eyes on me, but I didn't let it bother me.

"May I point out that you're here as well on a Friday night, after closing hours," he said with venom in his voice. I didn't even turn around. Of course I was here, I owned the joint!

"You can go now, Jason. We're done here," I said as I opened the outside door real wide for him and his ego to fit through.

He took the bait and walked out of the library, stopping just before leaving the building entirely. He leaned closely to me and said, "You're wrong, Emmeline Bailey. You don't know a thing about me or what I do for this town. I would explain it to you, but it seems I would be wasting my time with you. You don't trust people or let anyone into your life."

I took a deep, sharp intake of breath. That hurt. A lot.

He was right, though. I never let anyone into my life. I constantly ran away from all of my problems. How the hell did he know that?

I didn't inhale until he was pulling out of the driveway. Jason Ridgewell was not nice.

Twenty-Eight

The next day wasn't so easy for me. Due to many things, really, but the biggest one was lack of sleep. I was up most of the night tossing and turning. Regret over my decision to leave kept me awake like a wide-eyed owl. I hated that Jason Ridgewell had disrupted my plans. Actually I hated *him*.

I sat at my Gram's oak kitchen table and sipped my second cup of coffee when Tarryn and Becca strolled through the door. Both girls looked fresh-faced and beautiful. I was jealous.

Becca took one look at me and cringed, without meaning to I'm sure.

"Thanks, a lot, Becca," I snapped. Closing my eyes I realized I was way too harsh. "Sorry. Bad morning."

She sat down with me and said, "I can tell. Can I be of any help?"

I shook my head. "No. Thank you, though. I had a run in with that guy that wants to buy the library."

Tarryn joined us with a fresh cup of coffee in her hand.

"What! You actually met him?"

I nodded. "He came in here last night, saying he wanted a book. Long story short, he's related to Jack."

Both girls gave me shocked looks that made me almost laugh. Almost.

"How is that possible?" Tarryn asked as she sipped her coffee.

"Jack founded Bay Ridge, and Jason is his relation. I know it sounds weirdly coincidental, but it is really just tough luck."

Becca laughed, "Sounds more like fate to me. Is he cute?"

Leave it to happy-relationship-Becca to think that meeting Jason was fate.

"Well," I started. "He actually looks just like Jack. I mean, they could be twins. So yeah, he's very cute. But his attitude is deplorable."

Tarryn's smile grew and she nudged Becca in the arm. "It's gotta be fate. I agree with Bec."

I didn't agree. I told the girls how he came into the library all suave and asked for his dictionary. I didn't however explain to them my plans to leave. I could do that later. It was for the best that I didn't tell them while I was so tired. Seeing them so happy kept my spirits high and woke me up a little. If I told them my plans, it would make me feel like crap again.

"Well, I have to go to work," Becca announced, as she stood up. "I hate to leave though. All this good gossip and all." She leaned down and gave me a huge hug. "Tonight, there is a bon-fire on the beach. Will you come?"

I could use a night out of this place; a break from all that was on my mind.

"Yeah, I'll be there."

****

Tarryn was throwing clothes at me to try on. Her style was more punk-rock than mine, but she did have some cute ensembles that I could pull off.

"You need to dress more like the young, hot girl you are and less like a librarian," she stated as she tossed me a black lacy tank-top. "Not that you aren't still beautiful."

I looked down at the outfit I was currently wearing and back up to the clothes in my closet. I never wore the button down shirt I had on while I was in California. In fact, I hadn't ever worn any of the old outfits I used to. I dug through the closet, looking for all of my old clothes. When I moved in, I hadn't unpacked them all. I only got out the professional looking clothes, so that I would look like I belonged in the library. So that I looked like a librarian.

When I pulled out the huge box labelled *Emme's Shit* I laughed at the fact that my friends in Cali had labelled it for me. They weren't true friends, I knew that now, but they did have good senses of humor.

"What do you got there?" Tarryn asked, curiously.

"My clothes," I said as I pulled out my jeans, skirts, dresses, and sexy tops. "What about this?"

I asked as I pulled out my favorite white crop-top cami that had lace on the sides and my jeans.

"Now that's the perfect outfit for a bonfire," Tarryn said with a whistle. "You're going to look amazing. I don't know why you don't dress like that more often. Were you hiding the real you in there this whole time?"

She probably was joking around with the question, but she was absolutely right. I had stowed away the real me inside this closet. I wasn't sure why I felt the need to do that, but I wasn't going to hide her any longer.

"Yeah, I guess I was. It's time Emme comes back out to

play."

I changed into the outfit and threw on a pair of cute sandals. I decided a sexy bun with some loose curls looked best. I remember Harmony teaching me to do the very same thing at my first college party.

I was going to stop being a secluded librarian who only had fun when she opened a book. It was time to let loose for a little bit.

We got to the bonfire, and it was packed. I didn't know where the hell all these young beautiful people had come from because I had never seem them before. They were drinking and playing loud music that I loved. Suddenly, I had the urge to stay in this town. Maybe I should have been going out with Tarryn and Becca instead of staying in and pining over my book boyfriend. There was a whole world out here that I was missing out on. I met Jack and my life was totally in shambles. I had been back to Maine since last winter and I had nothing to show for it. My whole life was passing me by and I wasn't in the driver's seat.

I grabbed a beer from one of the coolers and cracked it open. I needed this night so I could get over him.

"Hey, did you pay for that beer?" A guy asked me with snarky tone. I turned around and came face to face with Jason, again.

"I did pay for it, actually." I gave the guy manning the cooler my five bucks. Jason was just going to torment me and ruin this night, wasn't he? "Are you following me now?"

He laughed and took a long drink of his own beer. "No, actually this bonfire was my idea."

Bullshit.

"Yeah, okay." I nodded and turned away from him.

He reached out and grabbed my arm, lightly. "Emmeline,

please hear me out."

I stopped and looked at him with my calculating gaze.

"Why should I, huh? I'm not here to discuss my business with you. I am actually getting over something, and I just want to have a little fun tonight, if that's all right with you."

I was expecting there to be a smile on his face, but instead there was actual concern. It was then that I saw some small differences between his face and Jack's. His eyebrows were a little lighter in color, almost blond, matching his lighter sandy blond hair. And his eyes weren't as blue as Jack's, but they were pretty stunning in the light of the fire. He also had light freckles that spotted across his nose and cheeks, barely discernable unless you were standing real close, which I was.

"I'm sorry about that. I don't want to talk business with you. I'm done asking you about your place. I promise to never again ask you to sell it to me."

I uncrossed my arms and felt myself relax.

"Okay, fine. Then what do you want to tell me?"

Unexpectedly, he grabbed my hand and pulled me away from the crowd of people where some chairs were already sitting. I looked back at my friends to see if they were okay, and they were, dancing with one another and having a good time.

I sat down, and Jason did as well, letting go of my hand. Strangely I didn't want him to.

What the hell is wrong with me? This guy is the enemy.

"I'm not the guy you think I am," he began, as he looked out toward the ocean. "I have friends. I just care about my job. I love what I do, and before you trash it, let me explain it to you."

I rolled my eyes a little.

"Fine. I'm listening," I told him, taking a huge sip of beer and relishing the slight buzz I already had.

"I was born into this job. JR Builders is my father's business, Jerome Ridgewell. He is a phenomenal builder. He can make a house into a home, if that makes sense."

It did. Many houses looked great on the outside, but once you went inside, it was cold and uninviting. Places like Gram's apartment didn't look like a house, but it felt comfortable and warm inside. It was home.

"I went to school for business because I didn't want to build homes. I wanted to go see the country, not be stuck here forever."

"That sounds familiar," I told him. "I got out of here as soon as I could."

He laughed and nudged me.

"So did I. But here we sit. I took over Dad's business when he needed me because my brother couldn't. He married a girl from Alaska and headed out there. So I became the business part of the company," he explained. We had a lot in common already. "We don't tear down historical buildings. We actually preserve what we can."

I preserved history, too. Or I used to.

"How is tearing down the old general store and making it a shopping mall preservation?"

"That general store is still standing, but in a different location. It's now the auto parts shop. We build malls because that's what the town needs. When Jackson Jr. built this town, he did so to create stability and jobs. What we had here before I came back from college was not what Jackson wanted. Many were out of work and couldn't provide for their families."

I watched Jason as he talked about this town and the light in his eyes brightened. It was then that I saw that he wasn't the enemy I had made him out to be. No, he wasn't a bad guy at all. He had dreams, just like Jack did, for this town. And I realized that he was going to be the one who made Bay Ridge what Jack always wanted: a place where people grew and raised their families. Bay Ridge was always a small fishing town that no one had ever heard of, but lately there were more houses being built and more people visiting from out of town.

Bay Ridge was becoming a place I didn't want to leave.

Twenty-Nine

Jason kept talking about his plans for Bay Ridge and how he wanted to make it a place where people could grow old and have all the amenities as any other town. While he spoke, I watched the partygoers laugh and be free surrounded by the flickering flames of the bonfire. The waves crashed in the backdrop and their laughter was actually louder. It was apparent that they loved life. They loved their lives here in Bay Ridge.

"I thought it was crazy that we had to drive an hour to go to the mall. Or that our high school was so old it has asbestos," Jason went on. "It's currently shut down because my father and I fought long and hard with town hall to get it rebuilt. The high school kids are attending the middle school for class. Crazy, isn't it?"

I nodded. "It is."

I was wrong about Jason. So wrong. He wasn't trying to hurt Gram's place, he was trying to build up the community and do better by the people here. He truly did honor Jack's memory.

"I'm sorry," I blurted aloud. My cheeks flamed red and

I nervously played with my hair. I wound the curls that hung down around my fingers.

"Sorry for what?"

I sighed. "For judging you so harshly without knowing you."

He sat back into the chair and sipped his drink. "I judged you, too, Emme. I am just as guilty as you are. You know what's funny?"

I turned to face him and said, "No, what?"

"I thought you were this mean, bitter girl when we spoke on the phone. But when I saw you in the library, I knew I was wrong. The girl I saw there was beautiful, not bitter. I could see then that you were holding onto a memory and you weren't mean at all. I also learned you're full of sass. I like it."

He called me beautiful. He also called me bitter and mean, but I ignored that because last night I said some pretty mean things myself. I had actually thought I hated him. I was so glad to be wrong about that.

"I think we both were wrong about one another," I concluded. "So, now what?"

He smiled at me, this sexy smile, so much like Jack's yet so different.

"Now we dance." He pulled me from my seat and into the wild dancing crowd. I let myself feel free and dance with Jason. He moved around me and placed his hands on my hips as we swayed to the music. When the song slowed, he pulled me closer, ever so gently. Jason and I fit together so well. My hands slid into his and my body glided against him as we danced slowly.

A huge part of me felt extremely guilty that I was starting to flirt with Jason, but another part told me that maybe Becca was right. Maybe fate did bring us together. It couldn't be coincidental that I met and connected to him. For that brief moment in my life, I let myself feel free.

The music had ended and the fire died down. Becca and Tarryn had gone home hours before, and I stayed with Jason talking until the very last partier found their safe ride home. Jason was the nicest guy I'd ever met in Bay Ridge. He wasn't like most of the guys I had met while growing up here. I learned that he was twenty-three and he had gone to school in Massachusetts to earn his associates in business before he made his way back home. He had his own place on his parents' land, a small apartment, as he described it.

"I eventually want to build my own house here, but that will take a while," he explained. "What about you? What are Emme's plans for the future?"

I thought about it for a minute, and the idea of moving to England and actually telling him about it made me feel almost sick to my stomach.

"I wanted to move to England to finish school, but I...I don't know now," I admitted. He was the first person I was telling about this new plan. There was something about him that told me I could trust him. "I never wanted Gram's library, so the plan was to train Tarryn and let her take the reins while I went back to school. But saying it out loud makes it so wrong."

He kicked the sand in front of him and laughed a little.

"What?" There was something he wasn't telling me, I could tell.

"It sounds like you just realized that it's a bad idea to leave someone with *your* responsibilities. You said your grandmother left you the place and it was like a burden at first. How do you think Tarryn will feel when you leave?"

He was right. Tarryn would view it like I had at first. It

wasn't her library to take care of. We had bonded, her and me, while we ran it and I would be tarnishing that bond. I was using her, and I felt like utter shit about it.

"That doesn't mean that you can't go to England someday. Right?"

I nodded absently. "Walk me home?"

He grabbed the last of the trash and threw it in the bin. "Sure."

While we walked the short trek to my place, I could hear the sounds of Bay Ridge at night. The frogs singing in the bog, the owls hooting in the birch trees, and the waves crashing in the distance. It was the sounds of home, my home.

"I can't leave this place. No matter how badly I want to, it's a part of me," I admitted, breaking the silence.

"I can understand that, trust me," Jason said. "I mean, why would you want to leave? I have always been able to see detail in the beautiful things of life. And this part of Maine is beautiful, trust me."

My breath hitched, and I stopped walking. Jason turned around and looked back at me.

"What happened?"

"Nothing, it's just that I always say that same thing. Well, sort of the same thing."

He grabbed my hand and pulled me along with him toward the library. I looked down at our linked hands and laughed a little. If anyone would have told me I would be holding hands with the enemy, I would have told them to piss off. But here we were.

"If you can see beautiful things, then why on earth would you want to leave this place?" he asked, breaking my train of thought.

"I don't know, honestly. I think there was never anything

keeping me here, I guess."

He snickered. "Well, we just have to change that then, don't we?"

We made it to the library and the door was unlocked for me, thanks to Tarryn. Jason looked up at the building and sighed.

"What?"

His face turned businesslike and serious. "The structure, it's beautiful. This building is so gorgeous that when I was inside it the other day, I thought that I would never tear it down. It's too amazing."

I smiled because he saw everything that I saw when I was inside of it. The wood work inside was original as was the crown molding and cathedral ceilings. Nothing about this place was modern.

"I'd love to learn the history of this old place sometime," he said. "That is if you want to see me again."

I couldn't help but smile so big it made my cheeks hurt. In fact they were already sore from all the laughing and smiling I had done at the bonfire. Being in Jason's presence made me, dare I say, happy. Happier than I had been since the last time I saw Jack, even though I hated to admit it.

"I'd love to learn about the history of Bay Ridge, sometime."

He raised an eyebrow at me and asked, "So you really are learning about the founder then, huh?"

I nodded and bit my lip. "In a way, yes. Let's just say he interests me. I'd like to see whatever happened to him. Well, his life story."

There was no way to explain that I wanted to see if Jack was okay, without sounding like a stalker. He might ask why a girl my age would have any interest in old ghosts. What would be my answer?

But he bought my excuse as he leaned against the entrance to the building.

"Well, from what I heard he was a mean and nasty guy. He was always unhappy. He did great things, but he wasn't a people person."

No. Not my Jack. He wasn't those things. He was the exact opposite. I shook my head in dismay.

"Surely, you're mistaken." I caught myself. "I mean, I read that he was kind and wanted to do great things for the town. He had kids, right? I mean, he had to if you're here."

Jason laughed. "Yeah, he got married, but he kept her at arm's length. I guess he had a real bad broken heart once, so he never really let people in. She hated him for treating her the way he did. He never included her in anything. Treated her like real crap."

I choked back tears that threatened and blinked my eyes to fight them off. Hearing this pained me. Jack married, but he shut his wife out and was mean to everyone. It was all my fault. I had to go back and make things right with him. I couldn't let his life be like that; I had to right the wrongs. I just had to say goodnight to Jason without showing how upset I really was, so I forced a yawn.

"Oh, sorry." I yawned again. "I'm so tired all of a sudden."

I even stretched my arms for the full effect. Jason stood straight and put his hands into his pockets. "Well, I won't keep you any longer. Can I...can I call you sometime? You did tell me never to call again, you know?"

As badly as I wanted to go, Jason was so adorable and a part of me wanted to hang out with him until the sun came up.

"I'm really sorry about that, by the way," I told him.

"I give you full permission to call me again. In fact I look forward to it."

"Good," he said with a smile. He backed away and waved. "Goodnight, Emme."

I sighed like a tween girl with a crush as he got farther away. Jason did things to me that I never thought possible; he made me giddy, in a good way.

I placed my hand on my beating chest and realized my heart was no longer broken.

Thirty

I was standing in a library, one that was not my own. I hoped it was a library in Jack's house, but then again, who knew? It could be in someone's house that Jack was visiting, making this trip even more awkward than it should have been. I was here to fix what I did wrong, but Jack wasn't here.

I wasn't disappointed that he wasn't there, at first. The last time I saw him, he was telling me that he didn't love me. I wasn't looking forward to that again. I came here to set things right between us. He had turned into someone else after meeting me, and I couldn't have that. I recalled the last thing he said to me, *"I am going to live my life without you, Emmeline. Do not come back, understand?"*

And I defied him and came back. What could I say? I didn't like to listen.

I battled with the idea of searching for him, but I wasn't in the proper attire. No surprise there. I had come, once again, unprepared.

The door opened and there was no time to hide, so I hoped for the best.

"The library is usually a quiet, oh dear!" It wasn't Jack; it was a woman that I hoped to be his mother. Her gray curls were piled upon her head and her dress was a deep burgundy; she was beautiful and elegant. Her wide eyes looked startled at my appearance.

"Hello," I stated. There was no reason to freak out. If I did, then she would do the same. So my idea was to stay as calm as possible.

"Hello, dear. May I inquire as to who you are? I've not seen you here before," she asked so eloquently.

Think fast, Emme.

"Uh, I, uh," I stuttered before landing my eyes on a *Good Housekeeping* book. The girl on the cover was plain and homely, but had a huge smile on her face like she was happy to be cleaning the house. I copied her smile and said, "I'm here to clean the library. I was just hired today, by Mr. Ridgewell."

This seemed to ease the lady before me as she nodded slightly and turned to her guests, a group of women the same age as herself.

With a sigh she explained to them that the library wasn't available.

"We'll have to go into the sitting room, ladies."

She didn't give me another glance as she closed the door behind her, but she answered the question about my whereabouts. I was indeed in Jack's home.

I let out a breath after she left, not realizing that I was holding it. The last thing I needed was to be arrested and sent to jail for breaking and entering in this time. I never knew how long I would be here and spending that time in a cell wasn't preferable.

I wandered about the room, looking at all the books

and thinking about the time when Jack brought me into the library in his other home. We had grown so close in such a short time. Falling in love didn't have a time-frame, it just happened. For us, maybe fate had other plans.

It wasn't that I didn't love him anymore; it was more like I loved him so much I wanted a different future for him. He was better without me in his life, but I had to make him see that, too. Once he did, he would understand. Learning what I did about Jenny made me realize that intruding in Jack's life was wrong. I had a job to do, and I royally messed it up.

"What are you doing here, Emmeline?" Jack asked in a sharp tone behind me.

I twirled around and realized that this wasn't going to be as easy as I previously thought.

"I met your relative in my time, Jack," I began. Saying "hello" and "how are you" wasn't necessary. It was time to get to the point. "I learned about your future, Jack."

Jack fell into a large green velvet chair and took off his bowler hat. He ran his hand over his face that I now saw had grown a rather large beard and long side-burns.

"Is he a good lad?"

I nodded. "He is. He's doing right by the town you created and honoring not only your memory, but your wishes. I know you asked me not to come back, but—"

"Then, Emmeline," he said sharply, interrupting me, "why are you back?"

His eyes met mine and he looked tired.

"I came to fix this hole between us. That I created. I wanted to tell you about what sort of man you become, Jack. I don't want your hate for me to hurt your chances of happiness. You grow into a very bitter and angry man, Jack. You are just like the man you didn't want to become."

"Stop," he said quietly, but loud enough for me to hear. "Don't you dare say that I am like my father. I am not bitter nor am I angered."

I sat down across from him in a matching chair.

"You may not be yet, but that is what will happen to you. Jack, you're angry with me, I get it. I'm angry with myself. But I had to do it. Don't hate me because I wanted a different future for myself and for you."

His eyes tore away from mine, and I wanted to hold him against me, to feel his touch again. Instead, I refrained. He didn't love me. He had admitted that the last time we were together. I have had time to come to grips with the truth, but it was still hard to be in his presence without feeling all the hurt again.

"I came here to tell you that you have to open your heart to someone, eventually, Jack. I know that you didn't love me," I said as I choked back a sob. "But I did love you. Hell, I think I still do. I will let you get on with your life, but you have to live it to the fullest. You have to promise to love whoever you're with, with all your heart."

He rolled his eyes.

"I lied to you, Emmeline. When you left me, you broke my heart. You broke me in two."

So, Tarryn was right. He didn't mean what he said. He did love me, and he was only being cruel so I stayed away. I tried not to smile at the fact that he did love me like I did him and to focus on my task.

"And in doing so, Jack, I broke my own heart. Can't you see that?"

I reached across, what felt like a large divide, and took his hand in mine. I clenched my hand around his, but he didn't reciprocate. I could feel the tense anger inside his fingers.

"I never meant to do that to you. If I could change it, I would. You have to stop this, now. You have a chance at love, don't ruin that for yourself. I get that you pushed me away, but don't do that to everyone else in your life."

He sighed. "I had that chance with you, and it's gone now. I shall never love again. That's my solemn vow."

I shook my head in defiance. God, he was stubborn.

"No, Jack. Don't you see, in life we have small moments and we have a lot of them. Those small moments are what define us as human beings. They can break us, yes, but it's how we rebuild ourselves after that makes the difference." I hoped, no prayed, that what I was saying made sense to him. Tears ran down my face as I spoke. "I was but a small moment in your huge life, Jack. And you cannot let me be the only love you will experience. I can honestly say that you are my first love, but I hope that you won't be the last."

His eyes grew dark as he locked them with mine.

"You wish for me to fall in love with someone else? Does that mean you've found another?"

I shook my head and willed him to see it my way. To see that life for us wasn't over. We had full lives left to live and he was young, like me.

"Jack, I haven't found another. But I want you to. Can you see why?"

He stood fast and ripped his hand from mine, as if it hurt to touch me. I was failing here, big time.

"No, Emmeline. I cannot fathom why you would want that for me. When I fall in love for the first time, that's it. No other can replace you. I want you with me here, every night. To live in this home beside me."

I felt like we were running in circles and getting nowhere fast. He wasn't listening to reason, no matter what I said. I wondered if anything I said would get through to him. Was it awful of me that I got over our relationship so fast? Or was it the mature thing to do?

I liked to think that because I knew he would succeed without me, it was easier to move on. If I stayed and gave into my feelings, I could erase him from history.

"No, Jack. I'm too young to settle down and be a wife in this era. And you, you're too young to settle for *me*. Life is just beginning for us," I said between quiet tears. "This isn't easy for me to do. You have to see that. I have a duty to fulfill as a Librarian and it took me coming all the way here to see that I can't run away from that. And you can't run away from love, either."

Up until I said that to him, I wasn't sure what I was going to do with my future. Seeing Jack stuck in his ways made me see that I absolutely didn't want to be stuck on one possible future for myself. My life was beginning, and there were many possibilities for me.

"I won't let you waste away here in this big house all because of me," I said firmly. "You're acting like a stage one clinger, Jack, and you have to learn to get over me. Pretend you never met me, whatever you have to do. Focus on what's important."

I had to treat Jack like a stray dog that was better off without me, and dammit, I hated when that happened in movies. I hated when he did it to me. When he told me he didn't love me was his way of protecting me. Well how did it feel, Jack?

It really bothered me when people were mean to those they really cared for because they either couldn't love them enough or they were shitty human beings. I was probably acting like both at the present moment.

His hurt gaze wasn't lost on me as I moved away from him and moved toward the window.

"Just pretend you never met me, Jack. It's easier that way," I said, coldly. "You were right when I saw you the last time; I should have never come back."

I felt it, that pull from the other side and I closed my eyes ready to go back.

"No, Emmeline, don't go!"

Thirty-One

"So was he really hurt? And he really did love you?" Tarryn asked with concern. We were outside lying in the sunlight after closing the library before it hid behind the clouds. Our skin soaked up the vitamins and the warmth after a long work day. It could possibly be the last sunny day until the end of fall.

I was telling her about my trip back and how awful it was. I didn't tell her my original plans to leave Maine. I had cancelled everything that morning: college and moving. I would be staying in Maine because it was my home.

Gram would want me to stay, and she would have been sorely disappointed if I ran away from my problems, again. I imagined that she was out there listening to me and Tarryn talk. She would have loved my new friends, and I liked to think that she'd be proud of what we did for the library.

Even though Gram was gone, Tarryn, Becca, and Rose were my new family. I wouldn't be leaving my family ever again.

"He was more angry than hurt. It was the hardest thing I ever had to do," I said as I put on my sunglasses. I had come back and cried myself to sleep. In fact I did that for the last three nights straight. I was just now able to talk about it. "I wish there was a way to make this whole thing better for him. I think that going back helped, though."

She nodded like she didn't doubt it.

"I bet he was able to see that you weren't his only potential at happiness and he was able to be happy again, Emme. How will you find out?"

"I have a plan."

My plan was showing up in an hour, and I needed to get dressed and out of my clothes from work. Tarryn and I headed upstairs where she made plans for her night and I got dressed. I chose a pair of jeans to ward off the mosquito bites and a black T-shirt. I pulled my curls down from my ponytail and they fell nicely onto my shoulders, luckily.

I would admit that the prospect of hanging out with Jason made things with Jack easier. I didn't expect him to be a boyfriend, but he was a new friend. He gave me hope that Jack wasn't the only love I would be able to find. Even if things never went anywhere with Jason, I knew that I was doing something that I hardly did before: opened myself up. Jason knew Jack's history and I would be able to see, tonight, if Jack ever changed.

Jason's car reminded me of California. It smelled like coconut and leather, and for some reason it brought back memories of college days. He was taking me somewhere that he claimed to be a surprise, so I sat back and let him drive the windy cliff roads. I looked out toward the ocean as he talked about new renovation projects in the works. I thought it was interesting that we both were in the business of preservation.

"You look really pretty with your hair down," Jason said,

catching me off-guard.

I smiled with a blush growing on my cheeks. "Thank you. I don't wear it down much. Curly hair sucks."

"Nah, don't say that. I like it. A lot."

Jason was flirting with me and I liked it. *A lot.*

Now when I looked at him, I didn't see Jack so much. Instead I saw Jason and what made him different from Jack. I loved his light blond hair and how he brushed it up in a sort of wave on top of his head. I adored his laugh and all the jokes he liked to tell me while we were driving. This guy was seriously full of life and had many interesting stories to tell. It kept the drive interesting while killing all nervousness inside me.

Before long we were pulling into heavily wooded area that looked oddly familiar to me. I couldn't place it, but I knew that I had been here before as a child. The wild blackberries growing along the entrance struck something inside me. A memory perhaps? Yes, that was it.

It was a class field trip, before my parents died, and my teacher was excited to take us to a new museum that was now open to the public. I don't remember much about the trip, but I do remember telling my parents about the wild blackberries that we ate on our hike around the property.

We pulled into a parking space and I saw we were alone. The place was dead.

"We're here," he announced as he took off his seat belt.

"Is it closed?" I asked looking around for signs of life.

He laughed. "It's been closed down for years. But it's a project of mine to reopen it to the public. She'll be back and open for viewing in spring of next year, hopefully."

"Come on, I want to show you everything I can before it gets too dark."

I followed him down a long and windy pathway. The sun shone through the tops of the trees, and I knew it wouldn't be long until night was upon us. I hoped he had a flashlight because I wasn't going to find my way out of here without it.

Jason grabbed my hand in his and laced his fingers with mine. Being with him came so natural, yet I felt bad about it. It was like I could feel Jack's ghost with us, telling me to stop. I fought the feeling and held onto to Jason's hand.

We finally came to an opening in the trees where a beautiful house sat before us. I had seen this house on my field trip and one other time.

"I know this house," I said to him.

"You must have come here on a field trip; I did too when I was a kid. I loved it. When it was closed and I learned the history of it and how it meant so much to my family, I had to reopen it."

Jason pulled me along with him as we walked up to the big, beautiful Victorian home. I looked down at our hands and realized they looked good together. It wasn't lost on me how good it felt, but I tucked those feelings away.

Instead I focused on the structure before me. The blue of the house had long since worn away, but the original windows were intact as were all the doors.

"She's a real beauty, isn't she?"

I nodded but found it hard to speak. I wasn't just looking at any old house; I was looking at Jack's house. The very house I had seen him only three nights before. So much had changed since then. Time warped a lot of the home, and I could see why they closed it down. It's been falling apart over time.

"I've been working hard to bring her back up to code and have her reestablished as a historical site for our town.

People will be able to come and visit and do field trips like they used to. We need a little bit of history here still, don't you agree?"

I swallowed the lump of sorrow and pride in my throat. I was incredibly mournful now that I stood by the home where Jack lived and he wasn't here with me. Yet I felt pride that Jason was fixing this old house and making it into a place where people could visit.

They would be honoring Jack's name by learning about who he was, and I couldn't help but feel like I had contributed to making his story real and for bringing to light the man he really was.

"Do you want to see inside?" Jason asked as he let my hand go.

It felt weird without his hand in mine and slightly awkward, so I folded my hands together and said, "Yeah."

The inside was better looking than the outside, as this part had fresh paint and brand new flooring throughout. Pictures hung all over the walls of men and woman and even little children. I noticed several glass enclosures all over the foyer where books or relics were strewn about.

"We haven't found actual rooms to put those in yet, but we're getting there," Jason said, pointing to the books.

"Who is helping you with all this?" I asked as I peered into the glass cases.

"Mostly my mom and dad, but I do a lot of the work. They're swamped with their own stuff, ya know?"

I nodded absently as a book pulled my attention to it. The case held a small book open to a page that had Jack's name and some writing that I couldn't make out.

"What's this?"

Jason came over and said, "Oh, that's Jackson's journal.

We found it up in the old library hidden underneath the floorboards. Lucky we ripped up the flooring and found it, huh?"

His journal. Jack might have written about me in there and I eagerly wanted nothing more than to read it. I had to convince Jason to let me without alerting him and freaking him out. My original plan to see if meeting with Jack worked was to just merely ask Jason about Jack again. But this journal would tell me everything I needed to know without involving Jason.

"Jason," I began, carefully. "This would be something I'd love to look through, as the town librarian. I could learn so much about your family, and you know how much it interests me."

I felt guilty playing the whole "girl who bats her lashes" card, but I really had to read about Jack. I had to know if my going back to him worked out or not. There was no other way to know.

Jason smiled and pulled out his keyring full of keys. "Sure, Emme, I trust you. Just get it back to me in a week. Is that enough time?"

I would devour that thing in one sitting, was he kidding me? You didn't give a reader a book like that and not expect it to be read in one night.

"I'll give it back before then," I promised him. "What else can you show me?"

I clutched the book to my chest and walked the rest of the tour with Jason. My ears listened to him talk about all of the plans for the place, but my mind was on the diary.

And while I wasn't ready to leave Jason's company, I wanted to go to my nook and read this. I fought off the feeling and made myself calm down so I could pay attention, but

Jason noticed.

Of course he did, he was too smart not to.

"Well, I think I'll end the tour here and get you home. It's getting late and you look tired," he said concerned.

I felt bad, but he was right. I needed a coffee and my pj's because I had work to do.

"Sorry, Jason. I am a little tired."

He walked me out and locked up the house. At first I thought he was upset, but as we walked the pathway back and he pulled out a flashlight and grabbed my hand, I knew he wasn't. He was just being attentive to my needs.

Jason was a lot like Jack, yet he was this century's version. He would never replace Jack, but he was growing into someone I liked, a lot. I wanted to keep seeing him, and I felt guilty for wanting that. I made my peace with Jack three nights ago. Even if he didn't want to end things between us, I knew that I had said what was in my heart.

All I could do was hope that it would set in and Jack would remember what I said after he let go of all the hurt and anger he had inside of him.

Thirty-Two

I cuddled up in my nook and leaned down on the soft pillows and blankets that I had laid out. The lights in the library were all out except for the one I had on above my head. It was just enough light to brighten my nook.

I had the journal, my guidebook, and Jack's book with me. If all went well, I could seal his book tonight and make my final entries into the guidebook. Tarryn was upstairs having a little get-together with some friends and knew I needed time alone with the journal. She met Jason after he dropped me off and walked me to the door.

She was happy to see me with him, and after he left, she said, "He's a keeper. Hold on to him for sure, Emme."

I blushed just thinking about it. Jason *was* a great guy, but I couldn't think about a future with him until I saw Jack's fate. He asked me out again, and I told him yes, but I needed to finish this before we set plans.

I cracked open the pages of the book and immersed myself in Jack's stories. Before I knew it, I was pulled inside his journal, not like I would be with my historical book, but more like the fiction book I entered once.

I could have pulled off the ring and read it like any other book, but I much rather liked it this way. This way I was with him as he described the events of his life. It was like flying over him as I watched his life play out right in front of my very eyes.

And I did see his life. I saw everything that happened to him after he arrived in America and onward. I was feasting on the pages of his book and learning more about him than I had ever before. Like how he opened the bank and why he picked the location for his house. He also talked a great deal about his mother and father and friends he met along the way.

He did talk about me, which was strange to see played out, but he didn't go into great detail. Until the day I had last visited him came and I saw the two of us standing together in the library. I tore my eyes away from the book and looked away. Tears pooled in my eyes—this was harder than I thought it would be. I ripped the ring off of my finger and read the journal like normal.

March 23, 1893

Miss Bailey came to visit me for the last time. I find that our friendship has served its purpose and I will no longer be seeing her. I often find myself wishing that she had never come to me in England, for she is an insufferable woman that has turned my world upside down. I can't help but feel angry at her. I know it's wrong, but I can't stop myself.

It's time to move on in my life and do what I was meant to do with it. She did remind me of that: my purpose here.

I stopped and fought the urge to throw the book across the room. I hated that he called me *insufferable*, but I reminded myself that he was angry when he wrote it. He might have seen a different view later.

I kept reading and learning about Jack's history making this town. He continued to make progress and talked a lot about knowing loss and heartache. I hoped he was talking about losing his father, but I knew better.

Finally, I came to the entry about another woman. Her name was Lorraine, and I wanted to see her face so badly. I wanted to see the woman who would become his wife.

I put the ring back on and was immersed once again into his journal, walking side by side with the woman he would love forever.

Lorraine was beautiful. No, more than that, she was glamorous, much like the actresses in the twenties. Her blonde bombshell hair had a finger wave that fell across her face and her lips were bright red without lipstick. She had a smile that would stop you dead in your tracks and a kindness about her that radiated throughout the small yard where she stood with Jack.

When she looked at Jack, she looked at him like a woman in love. She was just what Jack deserved. I could only hope that she would be able to thaw his frozen heart.

He wrote about how beautiful she was and how everyone in the town thought they made a great pair, but never about how much he loved her.

I was thrown into another day, a day where church bells rang and Jack stood wearing a fancy brown suit that held a flower on the lapel.

It was his wedding day. I fought the feelings of jealousy inside me, telling myself that this was best. This was what Jack needed and she was perfect for him.

May 10, 1902

Today is the day that Lorraine Engel becomes my wife. I can't help but think that I am not the man for her. I don't deserve such a fine woman. She's done all she can to keep me happy, even loving my mother as her own. I feel as if Lorraine could do better. I am not the man she thinks I am.

My heart sank. He still wasn't happy. I tried to make him forget me and forget his heartbreak.

How could our short tryst be hurting him so badly? We barely knew one another, but we did feel strongly. I didn't deny that I missed him and that I felt strongly for him. But I let the knowledge of knowing what I could have done to him to mess up his future guide me. It was what healed my hurting heart. I didn't want my story to be like Jenny's. I refused to leave this world and for Jack's life to never be known just to make him happy.

I just wished he could see what I did. I tried to help him, but he refused to let go of his anger.

I read on and on as the night grew longer. Tarryn's party upstairs quieted down, and before I knew it, she was standing in front of me holding a flashlight.

I looked up from inside the pages of Jack's journal and I was now in my world.

"Hey," she said as she sat down with me in my nook. "Everyone left and I came down to see how you're doing?"

I sighed. "Not good. He's not any happier. He got married and has a child with her."

"Well, how does that make you feel? Do you hate her?"

I laughed. "No. Actually, she's sort of amazing. I'm able to follow along the pages as if I'm there with them, but not the same as when I'm actually with him. I can't talk to him."

She thought for a minute as if trying to get her mind around the idea.

"So, it's like watching a movie?"

I nodded. "Kind of. But I'm in the movie as it plays out in front of me. They can't see me or hear me."

She shivered. "That's a little creepy. Kind of like visiting with ghosts."

I shrugged. It was definitely an invasion of privacy, but I tried not to think about the fact that these people were, in fact, dead.

"He's awful to his wife, and he's never around to see his kid. It's not right."

"What are you going to do, Emme? You can't change his future and you can't seem to heal him either. It's a conundrum. Why don't you come upstairs and have a drink with me. You deserve a break."

I did deserve a break and I couldn't watch Jack's life any longer. I'd seen enough. He never became the nice guy I knew him to be. Instead he immersed himself in his work and left Lorraine alone basically.

"I'll be up in a bit, I just want to put these away in the office," I said as I emerged from my nook and stretched.

"Okay, I'll go lie on the couch until you get done."

The hidden room had become my office of all things Librarian. I had alphabetized all of the books my ancestors read through and even added Jack's book. I put pictures of Tarryn and me up on the wall along with the other Librarians. We deserved a place there now.

I slipped Jack's journal next to Jack's book, and as I shoved it on the shelf, another book came tumbling down. I knelt down and picked it up.

It was Grace's last book, the one I met her in. I realized

then that all the other finished books had seals along the edges, but this one didn't. I ran my fingers along the spine and realized then what I had to do. I wasn't going to change Jack's broken heart by going back and talking to him. I couldn't help him by doing that, but I could help him by changing everything from the very beginning. I had to talk to Grace and Mr. Lockhart first.

Thirty-Three

Lockhart smiled widely at me as I stumbled inside his time. He was sitting alone, on a veranda, sipping tea. "Emmeline, how lovely to see you," he said. "Tea?"

I laughed. It was so strange, but it was like he was expecting me. At the table sat a single tea-service, waiting for me.

I sat at the small table across from him. I looked out beyond the veranda and saw that we were not at the Ridgewell Manor but somewhere else.

"Where are we?" I dared to ask.

He chuckled. "You mean, *when* are we?"

"Yes, I suppose."

"Doesn't it look familiar to you?" He waved his hand and I looked again. We were in Maine sitting on a balcony that I never knew existed, before now, in the library's building.

"This is your perfume shop, correct?"

He laughed again. Lockhart was a happy guy, he sure liked to laugh.

"I have a confession to make. My perfume shop was just a cover. I actually have many science experiments going and have been performing those for some time now," he admitted. "This is the very place where I wrote the formula to time-travel. I learned that traveling through time was never going to work by just simply riding in a machine or, rather, willing yourself there. You needed a form of transportation and the safest way was by book."

I leaned in. I was so intrigued and felt so special to be learning all that Harold Lockhart created.

"I wrote the formula in the pages of a book to keep track of them. And merely by accident, after creating the stones all of you preservers wear, did I travel through time."

I was confused. "But if you wrote the pages in a plain book, then when did you travel to?"

He tapped his nose. "You caught on! You're very observant, Emmeline. You see, I didn't have any blank pages left, so I grabbed a book off of a shelf. It was my favorite book about Abraham Lincoln. I absently held the stone inside my hands as I wrote, and before I knew it, BAM!"

I jumped.

"I was sitting in a room next to him. I realized after meeting the man I admired that I had a gift. Not only to travel through time periods, but to meet our histories' finest leaders and mentors throughout the world. I could see all things built, the wonders of the world even. But I couldn't keep this gift secret. I had to share it and teach others to preserve these stories about these fine people.

"It was important that we find the truth in their histories and their lives. I knew we had to preserve the books in such a way that no one could just simply grab them off the shelves; they had to be kept in pristine condition. So I created The Librarians and their libraries. I trusted my dear friend, Grace Bailey, to keep my secret. She tried to travel and I was pleased that she could do it. I attributed that to her fine family upbringing. I trusted her to help me find others in her family who would do it as well. And we had our Librarians. The Bailey family women were the only women I trusted could hold this gift. Bailey women are strong, Emmeline. You hold a power within you to travel."

"After we travel, how does the truth become reported?" I asked.

"Well, you do know that when we travel the words are recorded on the pages, making them true recordings of our time there. Our job was simple: record the findings and report them to the Historical Society of Libraries. Sealing the books before they are sent ensures that the findings aren't breached."

Oh. I didn't know I was supposed to send my books away. I was still learning about the facts, and it seemed I had things to do.

"Someone will contact you when it's time to send your books to the HSL, Emmeline. Don't worry too much, my dear."

I sipped the now cold tea, but I didn't care. I had learned the hows and whys that have always bothered me about my family's gift. All from the man himself. Harold Lockhart was a fabulous man who had created a wonderful gift for my family.

I gulped and remembered why I had come in the first place. I hated to tell him. I felt ashamed.

"Emmeline, I know why you are here," he said, shocking me once again.

I looked up from my teacup. "How could you?"

"He laughed. I just do. I am a man of science, my dear, but I recognize the look of someone who has a burden. And you, you have that look," he said as he tapped the air and pointed at me. "Now tell me."

I took in a deep breath, nerves running through me, and I told him everything. Not keeping anything hidden, for fear that it might somehow alter his remedy for helping me. I needed to leave nothing out.

And Lockhart didn't judge me or gasp in shock at what I had done to alter Jack's life. Instead he only nodded and listened intently.

When I was done, he rang a little bell and a maid came around the corner and took our service away from the table. I never knew that he had maids, or could afford them, even. But Harold probably needed all the help he could get in keeping his life running. Scientists are often drowning in their own work, and maybe he was too.

When she disappeared around the corner, he got up from the table and held out his hand. I took it and he led me down a set of stairs without saying a word. I was dying to see what he thought or what he could do to help me, but I tried to be patient.

We came to a small room and I recognized it as what was now my office. He pulled a book off of the same shelf that was built into the wall in my office.

"This is how you're going to fix your situation, Emmeline. I think you know what you need to do, don't you?"

I didn't want to say it out loud, but I did know.

"I do."

"You will take this book and you will fix it now, Emmeline. You will change everything in doing this. And after you have done so, you will be back in your own time. I will make it so. Now, you must go."

I took the book and held it against me. "Will I ever see

you again?"

He shrugged. "Maybe, maybe not. But remember this one thing."

"Yes?"

"We are there to observe, not to change. It's easy to get attached to these fine people, but you must be like a shadow. Moving alongside them, but never forming relationships with them. You can't be their friend, but you can be their acquaintance. You are there to learn, only."

I nodded. "I understand, sir."

"Good girl." He patted my arm. "Now, you best be on your way."

I pulled the book from my body and opened it.

****

I could see a floor and that I was lying on it. My face was smashed into it, along with bread crumbs and, there it was again, that darn rat poop. I sat up, this time not as slowly as the first.

The heat from the hot kitchen engulfed me again and I smiled. I stood up and saw her, the stout old woman with her hair in a loose bun. She looked at me in surprise and then shrieked, "Where did you come from, eh?"

"It's good to see you too, Nancy," I said with a smile.

"I have half a mind to grab my broom and whip you with it, lass. Don't you talk to me like you know me. Now, tell me who ya are and why you're in my kitchen."

I held up my hand with the ring on it and Nancy's eyes widened.

"Where did you get tha'?"

"I got it from Mr. Lockhart," I said, this time with full

confidence in my voice. "I've come to join your beautiful celebration of Jack's going away party."

She smiled and stepped back. "I never thought I'd see that ring again. Mr. Lockhart was a kind man. And that Miss Bailey, so beautiful."

"Yes, she was. Now, if you'd be so kind to help me change into something more fitting?"

She put her ladle down and helped me up the stairs. This time I knew where to go and I took off my clothes without any defiance. Nancy laced me up in a corset and pulled the same exact dress from the last time I was here, the mauve dress that took my breath away. I pulled it up and tried stepping into it, but she stopped me, again.

"I know, you'll do this part."

I let her help me into the dress and again she told me the story of the dress.

"This is the finest dress from France and was meant for Miss Everly to wear, but she passed last month."

This time I didn't need to ask how Miss Everly died because I recalled it was from a carriage accident.

I looked in the oval mirror that stood in the corner of the room. I looked like I was from the era; I looked elegant once again.

"Ah, now, aren't ya a pretty thing," Nancy said pulling me away from the mirror. "You can go down the stairs and join the party."

"I will be observing alongside the guests, Nancy. I'd like it if you held my secret like you did my great-grandmother's and Mr. Lockhart. I will go by *Mrs.* Bailey so that the men here think me to be married."

"Oh, yes, dearie. I understand, Mrs. it is."

I left the small room and took the back staircase, peering

around a corner until I found the right room. I wouldn't be hiding in the same room as before. This time I was going to be joining the guests. I found them all talking and sipping brandy in a large room with a gigantic fireplace.

I found a bunch of women and I joined in casual conversation. Things had to be different this time, much different, for this to work.

The women were speaking of the death of Miss Everly and how tremendously awful it was. I didn't chime in, but I did act solemn like they did. It wasn't hard blending in. They were a lot like the gossipy girls at my high school. You just had to nod and laugh at the right times.

"Ahem." A loud cough behind me startled me.

I turned and faced the man from which it came. Jackson Ridgewell Jr. had once again made himself known the same exact way as before.

"I don't think I've had the pleasure of an introduction," he said as he smiled at me with his beautiful grin.

"I'm Mrs. Bailey," I said with confidence. I couldn't falter, not even in the slightest. I had to stay strong and remember that this was the best thing for us, for him.

"How do you do Mrs. Bailey? I'm Jack—"

"Of course you are. I know who you are Mr. Ridgewell. This party is in your honor," I said. It felt fake, but I had a role to play. Always observe, never intrude.

He was still the epitome of hotness in a late twentieth century way. Being in his presence made my heart beat faster, still. I hated being dishonest with him, even if he didn't remember who I was.

"Do you have a first name, Mrs. Bailey?"

"Of course I do. It's Emmeline."

"What a beautiful name. Why are you in here alone?

Where is Mr. Bailey?"

My heart skipped a beat as I lied.

"My husband is in America. I came here on his behalf. He apologizes for not being able to attend. We wish you a safe trip, Mr. Ridgewell."

I smiled, and he took my hand and kissed it gently. "Thank you, Mrs. Bailey, for coming. I do hope you'll stay for dinner." He was totally flirting with me.

"Thank you, Jack. I will if I have time."

His smile grew large and he nodded. He pulled away from me and turned to walk away. I felt my heart die as he did.

What we had was now gone. I had changed our first meeting, and in doing so I had erased all memories we had made. They were gone from his mind and he would only ever know me as Mrs. Emmeline Bailey, if he remembered me at all. I, though, would never forget him and what we shared.

Jack Ridgewell taught me to love and to let down my guard. He taught me that I could let people into my life and even if that meant losing them, I would be all right. I had loved him and lost him, and I survived. I had become a better person, a stronger person, for it.

And I had known a love that was beautiful when I was with him. Jack's life would be better now. He would do all that he set out to do, but without the interference of me.

I watched him walk away, but before I turned to leave, he stopped. He turned around and looked at me, and said, "Mrs. Bailey, have we met before?"

I wanted nothing more than to tell him we had. Or that maybe in another life we would. Instead I said, "No, we haven't."

He laughed. "That's funny because you look familiar

somehow. And you called me, Jack. Only my friends call me Jack."

Shrugging, I replied, "Guess I'm your friend now, Jack."

He looked like he wanted to say something else, but he was bombarded by a man and his wife, thankfully. I had done what I needed to do.

It was time to leave. I felt the pull coming along just in time, and I walked out of the room and out of Jack's life. I wouldn't be coming back. Jack's story had been told, and I knew his future. There was no need for me to preserve it any longer.

Thirty-Four

Spring was in the air once again, and besides fall, it was a close favorite of mine. With the harsh winter gone, the colors of the trees came back. And life awoke once again. It seemed like life was flying by since I moved back home. Thinking about the winter I had first arrived made it feel like a lifetime ago. We had a bonfire with the crisp spring night air surrounding us. The fire rose and warmed us as we sat by it and ate our fill of pie and caramel apples that Becca brought from the coffee shop.

Rose drank her iced tea and told us how the building of her new office was going. She finally was getting what she needed for her career, and I was never as happy for her as I was then. Rose was a talented doctor and she was needed in this town.

I was still the librarian, and I wasn't going to be doing anything different anytime soon. I did decide to change my major, though, which didn't surprise Tarryn or Becca in the slightest, but Rose was shocked.

"I thought you wanted to be a teacher."

I laughed and sipped my coffee. "I did. I needed a

challenge though."

She side-eyed me. "Yeah, I'd say that getting your master's in Library Science will be a challenge for you."

I chucked my caramel apple at her and she dodged it.

"Hey! No wasting apples!" Becca yelled. "It took me forever to make those, you know?"

I held up my hands. "Sorry. But she made me." I pointed at Rose, who smiled guiltily.

"Aren't you going to be late, Emme?" Tarryn asked as she looked at her watch.

I checked the time, and she was right. I was going to be late. I got up from the chair and grabbed my coffee. "Time for me to head out."

Rose looked surprise. "What? Where are you going?"

"She has a date," Tarryn teased.

"With that hot construction guy?" Rose asked.

I laughed. "He's more than a *construction guy* and his name is Jason, remember?"

Rose had met him once at an end of the autumn party. I didn't expect her to remember the meeting since she got wasted that night.

I was still seeing Jason, but I asked him to not rush things. I couldn't fall head first into a relationship after everything I went through. I needed to go slowly and he understood.

"I'll see you girls later."

"Yep, we'll meet you there!" Tarryn called out.

"Don't forget to bring some of that pie, Becca," I reminded her.

"Why am I not invited?" Rose pouted.

"Aren't you on the clock?" I asked pointing to her scrubs. She giggled and sipped her tea.

"I'm on my lunch break. Have fun, Emme. Tell

construction guy I said, 'Hi.' "

I waved and got into my truck. The engine roared to life, and I took the streets with the windows down.

Gram would be proud of me for starting my life over like I did. I was proud of myself, too.

It wasn't easy starting over in Bay Ridge after college, but I did it. And it wasn't easy acclimating to the idea that I had a talent with books that no one else did in this town. I ran the library and was going back to school to be an official chronicler.

I missed Gram on nights like this. I even missed my parents. I wished they were all still with me, but since they weren't, I would do them proud. I would do the Bailey name proud, tonight and all the nights after this.

I pulled into the driveway, this time it wasn't dead, but full of cars.

The old Ridgewell home was lit up so bright you could see it from here. I got out and walked down the now finished walkway. The house wasn't up and running for business yet, but Jason was throwing a small party in celebration of getting the form of approval for historical preservation, which meant he would preserve the house with help from the Historical Society of Maine. His friends and family were gathered there to celebrate, and my friends would be joining in the party soon. I wanted to get here first though, before them. There was something I needed to do.

I stared at the beautiful home where Jack and his family lived. It was breathtaking.

Jason had done so much to it in these last several months, making it look just like new. Jack would have loved it.

"Emme, there you are," Jason said, coming out of the house and down the stairs. "I saw your car pull up."

He looked handsome. He always did, but tonight he looked less like the construction guy and more like the well-dressed man who had stepped into my library the first night. I didn't like to admit it, but he was really adorable that night, now that I think back on it. He had come in there to meet me, and looking at it now, he had to have been nervous. I wasn't nice to him on the phone. But he came there anyway. He took the risk.

I took the risk now, and I walked up to him and threw my arms around his neck and kissed him.

It wasn't a light kiss, but more like a ground shattering kiss. One that you never forgot.

He pulled back and said, "Wow. I don't know what I did to deserve that, but please do it again."

So I did.

Jason Ridgewell was making his way into my heart, even if I wanted things to slow down at first. I couldn't help but let him in. He was perfection, and I wouldn't let that slip out of my hands, not again.

I never looked at him and saw Jack anymore. Instead I saw the guy that was winning my heart with every word and every look.

We broke apart and he grabbed my hand. "Come on inside, beautiful. There are some people I want you to meet."

"Who?" I asked curiously.

"No one important, just my mom and dad."

I clenched his hand nervously. Was he serious? They were the most important.

"You are so gonna get it. This is trickery!" I said, jokingly.

"Maybe so. But I look forward to you getting back at me. When will that happen?"

I laughed. "You're naughty!"

"Yep. And you love me."

I stopped. "I do."

He looked at me seriously now. Not laughing or joking. "Do you? Love me?"

I shrugged my shoulders, nervously.

"Maybe I came here early to tell you that I love you." I smiled, trying to hide the nervousness that filled my whole body. I was shaking a little.

He faced me and placed his hands on my cheeks lightly, caressing me and softly said, "If you did, that would be fantastic because I love you, Emme."

He kissed me and pulled back too soon.

"We have people to meet, don't we?"

He sighed. "We do. I wish we could run off and be alone, but we have a whole house full of people who want to meet you, the famous librarian of Bay Ridge. I'm happy that you came here to tell me that."

"I'm glad you are. I was nervous."

He acted like it didn't matter. Like me telling him I loved him wasn't a big deal.

"I don't open up to people, Jason. But with you, I feel like I need to. I feel like we're going to be something important," I said. "And I didn't want to rush it."

"You can't rush things *that* important. But you also can't deny feelings this strong," he said matter-of-factly. "Now, we have people waiting for us."

I grabbed his hand and pulled him up the stairs.

"You better get to introducing me then, Mr. Ridgewell."

"I look forward to it."

I decided to take Gram's advice that she had given me the day we buried my parents. She told me to live my life and to be strong. That my parents gave me this life, as a gift, and I had to live each day, thankful for what I had and who I would be.

I was thankful for what I had and who was in my life now. I was also proud for who I became. I was a Librarian who could travel back in time and record history. I was given this gift by my family, and I intended to use it wisely from now on. In life we have small moments and we have a lot of them. Those small moments are what define us as human beings. They can break us, yes, but it's how we rebuild ourselves after that makes the difference.

The End

Acknowledgements

To CHBB, thank you for saying, "Yes" to The Librarian.
You saw something in this story and I am so glad you did.
To my Royals for quite possibly being the most amazing group of supporters ever.
To fans and readers that I've been blessed to have acquired over the years: Thank you for reading my books; for spending your hard earned money on them, and leaving reviews to help me grow as a writer. To my friends, family and daughters, thank you for seeing me for who I am and loving me.

The Author

Christy Sloat resides in New Jersey with her husband, two daughters and her Chihuahua, Sophie.

Christy has embraced the love of reading and writing since her youth and was inspired by her grandmother's loving support. She loves adventurous journeys with her friends and can be known to get lost inside a bookstore.

She is the Best Selling author of twelve novels including, The Visitors Series, The Past Lives Series and Slumber.

Christy Sloat
http://authorchristysloat.weebly.com

Printed in Great Britain
by Amazon